WOLVES OF THE
BEYOND

SHADOW WOLF

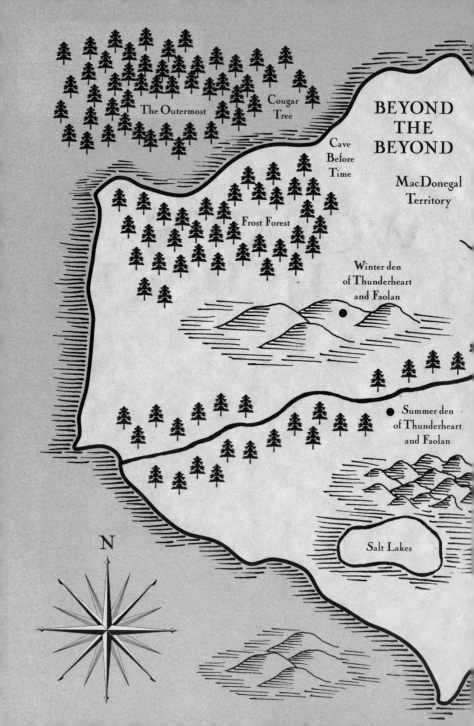

KATHRYN LASKY

WOLVES OF THE BEYOND

SHADOW WOLF

SCHOLASTIC INC.

New York Toronto London Auckland
Sydney Mexico City New Delhi Hong Kong

No part of this publication may be reproduced, stored in a retrieval system, or transmitted in any form or by any means, electronic, mechanical, photocopying, recording, or otherwise, without written permission of the publisher. For information regarding permission, write to Scholastic Inc., Attention: Permissions Department, 557 Broadway, New York, NY 10012.

This book was originally published in hardcover by Scholastic Press in 2010

ISBN 978-0-545-09313-2

12 11 10 9 8 7 6 5 4 3   12 13 14 15 16/0

Printed in the U.S.A.   40
This edition first printing, November 2011

Map illustration by Lillie Howard
Book design by Lillie Howard

For Mary Alice Kier and Anna Cottle—
The Fengos of my Watch

K.L.

CONTENTS

THE DARKEST
OF THE DARK

IT WAS THE SMELL OF GRASS —
late summer grass, clover water, and bitterroot with a
faint trace of ash. The vivid scents flowed through Faolan
like a river, stirring lost memories. *This is my pack, the
Pack of the Eastern Scree. This is my clan, the clan of
the MacDuncans.* Each smell seemed to reassure Faolan
that at last he was home.

A pack wolf's scent varied slightly depending upon
the season or what the wolf had eaten. But beneath these
small differences was an elemental scent, the essence of
them all. In his sleep, Faolan was wrapped safe and secure
in a blanket of these familiar and longed-for smells. He
was bound tight by the scent of the clan.

And yet Faolan was not in a pack den surrounded by
the warm, moist breathing of slumbering wolves. He was

alone. As a gnaw wolf, he was banished to sleep on the edges of the pack's territory. He must find whatever shelter he could. The rest of the pack had divided itself between two roomy dens they had excavated the previous summer on the Crooked Back Ridge, far from Faolan. But their scent lingered.

Faolan quivered. There were tiny cracks in his sleep through which horrors darker than this moonless night slid. The blackness suddenly was scored with flames. *Wake up! Wake up!* he shouted in his dream. But this was no dream; it was a memory. Even though he was asleep, Faolan could feel half a dozen packs from several clans hard on him, determined to run him into flames all because of his splayed paw. He could feel the heat of the flames as he leaped the wall of fire and jumped for the sun. Faolan thumped his paw on the ground he had dug for a den, and it was the noise and the small rain of dirt sifting down from the roof that finally woke him.

He rose up as far as he could in the tight confines of the hole. It was only in the darkest of the dark, on nights when the moon disappeared, that these terrors found their form. At those times, wolves seldom howled and it seemed to Faolan that the silence left spaces through which fear could slip.

He sniffed the air. There was not a trace of smoke or fire, only the lovely redolence of the pack's scent wafting through the dark. *My nose tells me I am home, I belong, this is my kin, my clan, and yet*... There was an ache deep inside Faolan that no scent could touch.

CHAPTER ONE

CARIBOU MOON

THERE WAS A TIME IN EARLY autumn when the moon cut the night like the thin curve of a caribou antler. It was at this time that the herds began to move south, first the cows with their calves and then the males. The wolves would track the beginnings of this great migration to seek out any old females or weak youngsters, but the hunting code of the clans forbade the killing of healthy calves. And the real hunting did not begin until the males came.

On this morning as the sun broke on the horizon, a howl curled into the air. It was the summoning howl of Greer, the she-wolf *skreeleen* of the MacDuncan River Pack. But it was not for caribou, it was for moose. The tracks of a bull moose had been discovered near the river. Scouts had been sent out to find the trail, and while they were gone, a *byrrgis*, the hunting formation, was gathering.

Bull moose could be unpredictable and, despite their staggering bulk, quite nimble. Therefore, it required a good-size *byrrgis* to bring them down. It was dangerous work, especially at this time of year, the moose mating season. Even Faolan's second milk mother, a grizzly bear, gave moose a wide margin during the time of the Caribou Moon. Faolan tried to keep calm as the packs gathered and waited for the scouts' return. He could hear the din of the *gaddergludder*, the pack rally that preceded the hunt of big game like moose. He felt a rush deep in his chest and pawed the ground.

This was his chance at last, he thought. He would hunt with the pack and he would get it right. There were so many rules and customs. The wolves had special words for so many things—pack words, clan words—and Faolan had been a packless, clanless wolf for the first year of his life. Because of his strangely splayed paw, he had been declared at birth a *malcadh*, a cursed pup. According to the rigid codes that governed the wolf clans of the Beyond, all *malcadhs* were cast out, taken by the Obea of a clan to be left to die or be devoured by other predators. The parents of the *malcadh* were also banished from the clan's territory and forbidden ever to mate with each other again. In this way, the bloodlines of the packs were kept healthy. In the very rare event a *malcadh* survived, he could return to the clan but only as a gnaw wolf, the lowest-ranking wolf of all.

Faolan had not died. He had been saved, rescued from the river by a grizzly bear, Thunderheart. For almost a year that he and the grizzly, his second Milk Giver, had stayed together. Then at the end of winter, she had died in the earthquake. Through the spring and most of the summer, Faolan had lived as a lone wolf. But less than a moon cycle ago, driven by loneliness, he had returned to the wolves. "Returned"—an odd word, for he had never lived long enough with the wolves to truly belong. And now, every minute of every day, he was reminded of that fact. Even the young pups in the pack constantly made fun of him. "Say 'caribou,' Faolan!" they would demand. Then when he said it, they yipped gleefully. "Sounds like a bear! Doesn't he?" They could tease him all they wanted because he was a gnaw wolf.

Lord Bhreac, leader of the Eastern Scree Pack, was approaching with his lieutenants. Quickly, Faolan tried to assume the posture of submission that was required whenever a pack member approached, particularly high-ranking wolves such as the pack lord. Before his belly had touched the ground, Faolan felt a sharp blow to his flank. *Not quick enough*, he thought.

It was Flint, a lieutenant, who had hit him and sent him sprawling. Flint was now coming back for a muzzle grab, one of the most humiliating and painful chops that could be delivered to a gnaw wolf.

"Don't waste your energy, Flint," Bhreac barked. "Let him be. You need your strength for the *byrrgis*."

What about me? Faolan thought. *Don't I need my strength as well?* He consoled himself with the thought that he would no longer be invisible when they saw him run in the *byrrgis*.

Bhreac paused and turned to look back at Faolan to make sure that he was following with his tail tucked between his legs in the slouching posture of a low-ranking wolf. "And remember. The bones will be big so we'll see how well you have learned your gnawing!"

Yes, the gnawing, but what about hunting? Faolan wondered. He could do so much more than simply gnaw a bone from which higher-ranking wolves had already stripped the meat. They would see what he could do on this *byrrgis*. They would see him run. The females of the pack were said to be the fastest runners, faster than males. *But they're not as fast as I am*, Faolan thought. And what wolf could walk on its hind legs? Thunderheart had taught him to do that. They hadn't seen it yet. Faolan wasn't sure if this peculiar talent would be necessary in a *byrrgis*, but if so — well, that would stop the other wolves in their tracks!

It was a fact that gnaw wolves were objects of general abuse. Marked by deformity, they became living symbols of the threat of bad blood, and it was as if the clan was somehow cleansing itself of taint through maltreatment of the gnaw wolves. Much was required of these gnaw wolves beyond serving as scapegoats. They were expected to learn to gnaw bones with a proficiency and delicacy that no ordinary wolf could match, keeping the chronicles of the wolf packs and clans of the Beyond on the bones they carved.

As he was being led away by Lord Bhreac, Faolan caught sight of a she-wolf full-bellied with pup.

"She's rather late in the season to be with a pup, is she not, Flint?" commented Bhreac.

"Indeed. And so often those wolves who carry late give birth too early. Let's hope she doesn't go *by-lang* with fear that it's a cursed one."

Faolan lagged a bit behind and turned to look at the

she-wolf. There was a nervous light in her eyes, and he saw another she-wolf with two pups diverge from her path to give the expectant mother a wide margin. One of the pups started to veer back, but his mother gave him a sharp cuff and growled, "Get away from her!"

Faolan's heart went out to the she-wolf. He hoped she hadn't heard, but he could tell from the way her head drooped that she had. It would be a wonder if she did not go *by-lang*. *A cursed one, they called the unborn pup,* Faolan thought. *As I was. As I am!* A malcadh. Had his first Milk Giver gone *by-lang*? Had she run off into the deep away to keep him safe from the laws of the clan?

CHAPTER TWO

CHALLENGING
THE ORDER

AS THEY APPROACHED THE BURN,
the site of the *gaddergludder*, where two dozen or more
members of the combined packs were gathering, Faolan
felt the stares of the other wolves. He heard murmurs of
astonishment as well. "He's too big for a gnaw wolf." "Too
well fed." "He must be sneaking meat at kills and not
waiting." "No pack wolf would permit..." "He's just
large...."

"Take a lesson from Heep over there," Lord Bhreac
said. "A model gnaw wolf!" Faolan had not yet met any of
the other gnaw wolves. Perhaps he could learn something
from Heep; the humility expected of a gnaw wolf did not
come easily to him. Faolan made his way to the top of the
Burn. Amid the tail wagging, bowing, and howling, he
spotted a tailless yellow wolf writhing in the dirt.

Faolan's submission postures left something to be desired. It was as if his knees simply could not bend enough; his shoulders seemed unready to flex so that he could drop to his belly; and he hated twisting his neck to press his face into the ground.

So this was what was considered a model gnaw wolf! Faolan felt sick. He had never seen a wolf grind himself so deeply into the ground. Heep's muzzle had disappeared into the dusty earth, and Faolan wondered how he could even breathe. Heep's eyes — more yellow than green — slid back into his head so that only the whites showed, but Faolan caught him glimpsing around every few seconds to see who was watching him. And all the while, Faolan noticed that the yellow wolf's hindquarters twitched, as if he were trying to shove his tail between his legs. But he had no tail to tuck in submission, wag in happiness, or hold out rigid in a display of dominance.

Heep wore this humility like a second pelt, and it gave Faolan a queasy feeling in his stomach. But Heep was supposed to be a model gnaw wolf, and perhaps he would tell Faolan something about the *byrrgis* and the hunt.

Faolan sank to his knees near Heep. "So when do we get to join in the howling?"

"What?" the yellow wolf rasped.

"I said, when do we —"

"I know what you said, gnaw wolf. I am simply astonished by the question! You know nothing, do you?"

"It was just a question. I don't know all the ways yet."

"At this rate, you never will," muttered Heep. "Gnaw wolves do not howl at *gaddergludders*. They do not howl at any pack or clan rallies."

Faolan was tempted to ask why but felt perhaps it was better not to. He did, however, want to know about the actual *byrrgis*. Forget howling about it. What was the hunt like?

"Can you tell me about the *byrrgis*? I can run…" He hesitated. He would not say he could run as fast as the females, since that might be inviting trouble. Instead, he said, "I have a lot of strength. I can run long and hard."

Heep raised his muzzle from the dirt and gave him a withering glance. "It really won't matter."

"What do you mean, it won't matter?"

At just that moment, Lord Claren walked by. He briefly paused in front of Heep and observed his writhings of submission, which seemed to stimulate Heep to even more frantic displays.

"So pleased to serve in my most humble way. Let the more noble wolves, the captain and the corporals of the *byrrgis*, be aided by my most humble efforts as a sweeper as I sniff the scat and urine of the prey. To accurately report on the condition of their droppings is a glory unto me if it serves the greater glory of the *byrrgis*."

Droppings! What was Heep talking about? That was their job, to sniff the *droppings*? Faolan was astonished. He had thought that, even though they were gnaw wolves and not permitted the first, second, or even tenth bite of prey after it had been brought down, they would not be relegated to sniffing droppings. Like a guttering flame, the anticipation Faolan had felt now flared and extinguished.

Heep slid his eyes toward Faolan and whispered, "That is indeed our task, gnaw wolf—to sniff the scat of the prey. No more. No running to speak of, nor are we part of the kill rush at the end. We sniff scat," he said, turning to Lord Claren, who nodded approvingly at Heep's explanation.

"And I would not deem you too proud, Lord Claren," Heep continued, "if you chose to avoid me for some time after this most magnificent hunt because of the stench I shall have acquired in the performance of my task." He paused in this fawning litany of self-abasement and added a small, delicate writhe. "Know that I am filled with humility at the mere chance of serving thus, and I shall wear the stench as a badge of my most humble service."

Lord Claren walked away. As soon as he was out of earshot, Faolan said, "Heep."

"What is it now, gnaw wolf?" Heep replied.

"Can't you call me by my name—Faolan?"

"You haven't earned that name." Heep's nostrils pinched together and he spoke with obvious disdain.

"It is the name given to me by my second Milk Giver."

"Oh!" Heep said. "That bear."

"Yes, that bear, the grizzly Thunderheart!"

Heep took a step closer. "Let me explain something to you, gnaw wolf. There is no such thing as a Milk Giver, first, second, or third, for a *malcadh*. Whoever this so-called Milk Giver was, she is no better than an impostor. And you show only stupidity and arrogance in thinking otherwise."

Faolan growled and stepped closer, which seemed to surprise Heep. As a longer-serving gnaw wolf in a pack, Heep had seniority and had not expected to be approached in such a manner.

"Urskadamus!" Faolan muttered the old bear curse he had learned from Thunderheart. He heard some she-wolves snicker, but he didn't pay any attention and turned away from the gnaw wolf.

Faolan realized that a wolf had been observing him

from across the way. She was young, tawny colored, about his age, he thought, but smaller and certainly not a gnaw wolf. Not when she was so well fed and had no trace of a deformity.

She was looking at him curiously. He could not return her gaze. It would be considered an affront for a gnaw wolf to look directly at another wolf, even if that wolf were the same age. But out of the corner of his eye, he could see that she was approaching him cautiously. He must sink lower, lay back his ears, and try as best he could to twist his neck and shove his face into the ground. Her words came softly and surprised him.

"It's hard for you, isn't it?" Somehow he knew immediately what she meant. "You can't pretend, can you? Not like Heep."

"Not like Heep. No wolf could be like him. He hardly seems a wolf to me."

"Maybe not, but sometimes you have to pretend. This is easy compared to—"

"Compared to what?"

"Shhh! Here he comes."

Heep came slithering on his belly back toward them. "Oh, my, that such a proud and noble young wolf should speak to humble creatures as ourselves. Such a gifted young she-wolf from the noble Carreg Gaer of our chieftain Duncan MacDuncan deigns to speak with the likes of us!"

Carreg Gaer! So she was not from the River Pack, Faolan thought. Carreg Gaer was the term used for the pack of the chieftain. But why was she here? It seemed as if she was embarrassed by Heep's lavish display of humiliation, and she turned away to join the *gaddergludder*. Soon the *skreeleen's* voice rose to a high pitch as she howled the final summoning call.

"To the Marrow!"

The two packs raced off to the north.

There were always two flanks in a *byrrgis* formation, either east and west or north and south. If there was just one gnaw wolf, that wolf was required to cover both flanks. With two, Faolan had been assigned the eastern flank, considered the inferior flank because of an old superstition. Heep was the sweeper on the west, and together they were the very last in the line of the thirty-two wolves that comprised the *byrrgis*.

The *byrrgis* stretched out over half a league as it climbed a steep incline. They were traveling at an exasperatingly slow speed. But Faolan knew he must stay in position. The first pile of droppings appeared and he diligently sniffed it. He was making his way up to report the scent to the sublieutenant, a large male named Donegal, when Heep appeared. "I'll be obliged to report that."

"But why? I got the scent." And before Faolan spoke next, he eyed Heep carefully. "Although I am even lower than you as a new gnaw wolf, I think that if you reported this, it would be considered most...most un-humble for the scent finder to have another report from the western flank."

Heep raised his yellow eyes. There seemed barely a trace of the luminous green that suffused the eyes of the wolves of the Beyond.

"You don't say," he replied softly.

"I do say. You might provoke the sublieutenant, for your nose is dry, and not damp with the steam of moose dung."

The yellow wolf began to walk away but turned once and gave Faolan a baleful look.

After Faolan reported to the sublieutenant, he and Heep were the last to reach the top of a rise. This gave them a good view of the *byrrgis* on the flats as it accelerated from what was known as press-paw speed to attack speed. It was as if a wave passed through the *byrrgis* at the moment of acceleration. The nearly three dozen wolves worked as one, their minds, their spirits, and their muscles merged. They didn't need to think, they didn't need to bark, for they belonged together, pressed between earth and sky like streaking clouds racing low on the horizon.

Faolan blinked as he saw the young tawny she-wolf flash out from behind an outflanker. Until prey came into closing range, the outflankers hung back. Once the point wolf thought the prey was beginning to tire, the outflankers streaked out to run.

How Faolan envied the young wolf from the Carreg Gaer. He could almost feel her muscles as her tawny body stretched. Her neck seemed endlessly long. Threads of saliva spun from her mouth as she ran, and yet it appeared so effortless. Faolan wanted to be a part of this. He could do this. He knew he could. He had picked off a caribou from a herd by himself just moons before.

Faolan saw Heep scurrying ahead. He must have found some droppings or perhaps a pool of urine. Well, let him have the "honor" of reporting to the sublieutenant.

The image of those streaking wolves spurred Faolan to charge ahead. He kicked up a whirlwind of dust with his hind legs as he sprang forward. The entire eastern flank had contracted into one tight unit that suddenly increased its speed. Faolan was not sure exactly why they were doing this, but he wanted to be a part of it. No one would notice if he sped up and packed in with them.

Seconds later, some sort of signal passed, and he felt the pressure of the wolves compacting around him. He was becoming one of them! He felt it in his marrow. Like metal in the heat of the forge, he was changing. His pace melded with theirs, his muscle became part of a larger one, his heart pumped, joining the single rhythm of all the hearts of all these wolves. He was a member of the *byrrgis*! A deep thrill coursed through him.

But what is happening now? he wondered as he sensed a change in direction. The bull moose was turning sharply to the north. This could not be right, for it seemed as if they might be driving the moose into rocky terrain that held a maze of gullies through which he could escape. Faolan put on a new burst of speed. The time might be coming, he thought with overwhelming excitement, for him to rise up on his hind legs. He could stop this bull in seconds! He cut out from the press of wolves and blasted forward so he could get ahead of the moose.

At the moment Faolan decided to break out, Heep noticed a whirlwind of rising dust. *What in the name of Lupus?* he thought, and purposely lagged just a bit behind in his position so he could edge over for a better view of the eastern flank. He blinked. He simply could not believe what he was seeing. Obviously, Faolan had no idea that the *byrrgis* was executing a crimping maneuver, designed to turn the moose. With his silvery tail floating out behind him like a plume, Faolan was streaking ahead and actually crimping the crimpers. This was an unimaginable violation of the *byrrgnock* laws—a first-degree offense.

A deep thrill coursed through the yellow wolf. By the Moon of the Singing Grass, this wolf would be out of the pack, out of the clan, and heading for the Dim World! The yellow wolf did not have to utter a word. Didn't have to do a thing. The gnaw wolf Faolan was stripping his own bones!

Faolan was running full throttle. He stretched out, feeling the wind through his fur and the ground so light beneath his feet. He knew that this was what he was made for—to catch the wind, to bite the sun that was dropping behind the horizon. The tawny haunches of the young female were drawing into view. It surprised him that he had devoured so much distance so fast. He felt the power in his muscles.

As Faolan closed in on the front-runners, he began to pick up signals that were flying back and forth between the corporals and the captains. Subtle motions, gestures—a flick of an ear, a sudden up-tip of a tail. He saw the signals but did not know their meaning. So when

Faolan streaked out ahead of the pack, ahead of the out-flankers, ahead of the point wolves, he did not hear the muffled dissonance as the pace was broken, nor the baffled, low growls of the two packs behind him. He was thinking of what was ahead—the huge bull moose he was going to stop. Faolan pulled ahead of the moose, out far enough in front to spin around and rise up on his back legs. He felt the spirit of the grizzly bear Thunderheart flow through him as he lifted up. He held his forepaws just like Thunderheart held hers, and it was as if he could feel his claws growing longer, sharper. *I am a wolf and a bear—a grizzly bear.* His howl crashed like thunder.

The moose skidded to a halt. A wild light filled his dark eyes as he took in the confounding sight before him. Then the moose bellowed and wheeled about—to charge the *byrrgis*! It was as if a mountain tore through the thirty-one wolves. There was a clamorous burst of howls and shrieks.

Great Ursus, what have I done?

But Faolan knew without being told. He had disturbed the order. A gnaw wolf had dared to cut out of the *byrrgis* and run beyond the outflankers! Beyond the point wolves! The *byrrgis* had been broken, and the bull moose had escaped.

CHAPTER THREE

THE OUTFLANKER'S RAGE

HE EXPECTED PUNISHMENT. AFTER all, that was what gnaw wolves were made for. They got random nips if they came too close to a carcass before the appropriate time, shunnings, often a wallop on their muzzles, and of course they served as the butt of all jokes and pranks. This he could have endured and did endure. But when he was told that Heep would be called to gnaw the bone recording Faolan's breach of conduct as well as deliver the gnaw bite, Faolan felt nausea rise up in him.

He had spoiled the hunt. He was guilty of one of the most serious infractions of the code of laws that governed so many aspects of the wolves' lives. He had cracked the *byrrgis*, and even if the wolves had been able to reassemble, they would not chase the moose. Meat gotten through a disturbance of the order was not considered *morrin.* Indeed, it was declared *cag mag*, an old wolf word for tainted meat, and since tainted meat was thought to make one insane, the expression also meant "going crazy."

But it was not just the meat that was *cag mag*. From the malevolent looks the wolves were giving him, Faolan knew they thought he was tainted, too. He heard their whispers. "He's more bear than wolf," one male said to his mate.

"And we," the mate replied, "have to go hungry because of him!"

But their words were nothing compared to what was coming. Faolan felt his marrow freeze when he saw the tawny wolf, the young outflanker called Mhairie, approaching. He sank to the ground. And oddly enough, the dirt hit his belly faster than it ever had before. He shoved his face into the grit, but before he could utter the first sound of an apology, her words were upon him like a swarm of stinging bees.

"What were you thinking? You wrecked my chance. Do you know how many she-wolves my age are ever asked to run as an outflanker?" She did not wait for an answer. "Of course not. You know nothing. You are an absolute idiot!"

"I know, I know," he said, his voice hoarse with desperation.

"We're going hungry and that's the least of it. We're lucky no wolves were killed when that moose charged."

"Look—I think I should just go away. They'll out-clan me for sure and then—"

But Mhairie cut him off. "Duncan MacDuncan decides that, not you!" she spat.

"Well, why stay around?"

"Why stay around? Look, you mealy-marrowed piece of scat. You have to go to the Carreg Gaer and have a hearing by the *raghnaid*. You can stand up to a moose on your stupid hind legs and prance about like a bear, but you can't face our court of justice? And just where were you thinking of going?"

"Um..." He hesitated.

"Where? Ga'Hoole, I suppose?"

"The thought had crossed my mind," Faolan muttered.

There was complete silence, a stunned silence. Slowly, Mhairie began to speak. "Are you blazed? Moon blinked? Have your brains gone *cag mag*?"

"It was just an idea," Faolan said, trying to drive his

face farther into the dirt while rolling back his eyes so he could see her.

"Great Lupus, you are pathetic! You don't even know how to do the third-stage submission roll, which, incidently, you are supposed to be doing right now after the initial belly scrape. You don't know that, let alone anything else about our world. You think you're just going to *churrlulu* your way through this."

"I don't know what *churrlulu* means," Faolan admitted.

"My point exactly! *Churrlulu* is the owl word for laughing something off, taking it lightly. Go to Ga'Hoole. You don't speak the language. You don't fly."

"I know some owl words. I had a friend, an owl, a Rogue smith."

"Oh, fantastic. You had a friend, a Rogue smith," Mhairie sneered, then cocked her head. "Forget Ga'Hoole. You don't belong there."

"Well, I don't belong here!" Faolan answered. He tried to keep his ears laid flat as was proper, but they kept twitching up.

Mhairie sighed. "I still can't believe what you did on that *byrrgis*. I mean, for the love of Lupus, this was supposed to be my...my..." Mhairie began to stammer. "My big moment. I could have finished the crimp if it hadn't been for you.

"Look, I don't know what the *raghnaid* will do. I'm not sure when they'll call you. Not with Duncan…" She started again. "Not with Duncan MacDuncan so…so sick." Her voice dwindled to an aching whisper. But within seconds, the sting was back.

"And one more thing—that tone of yours! You don't use that tone with me or with any other wolf. You are a gnaw wolf. Everyone knows that you have incredible strength. They saw you jump the fire trap. Wolves are superstitious. There are a lot who think you challenged the order when you jumped that wall of flames. Fractured the Great Chain. But that was survival. Mere survival. Just don't go around mouthing off and asking insolent questions!"

Why would she say "mere" survival? Faolan wondered. There was nothing small about being hunted down by a *byrrgis* and jumping over a wall of towering flames.

"What you did in the moose hunt confirms what a lot of these wolves thought back then when you jumped the fire trap. They want you out. They think you'll bring moon rot. No, not just bring it—that you *are* it. You are walking moon rot."

"They really believe that?" Faolan was bewildered. Moon rot was the shadow cast during the day by the previous night's moon. It was believed to be an ill omen.

"It's no excuse that you were a lone wolf and don't know the ways of the pack, of the clan. You show no inclination for learning them. Absolutely none whatsoever!"

"But what's the sense of it all? Lupus gave me strong legs. I learned to jump, to run, and it's all wasted here. I can't do any of what I learned—why not?"

"You think it's all about you, Faolan, just you. Well, it isn't. The pack is not a single wolf. The clan is not a single pack." Mhairie flashed him a last angry glance. "As you'll learn when you face the *raghnaid*."

Faolan's tail instinctively twitched between his legs. The *raghnaid* was awaiting him, and his biggest humiliation yet.

CHAPTER FOUR

THE PRINT
IN THE MUD

THE GNAW BITE WAS A PUNISHMENT
seldom administered. But the high-ranking members of
the pack agreed that the infraction of the laws of the *byrrgis* was so serious that Faolan must be bitten. To add insult
to injury, Heep was chosen to inflict the bite. Lord Claren,
head of the River Pack, and Lord Bhreac of the Pack of
the Eastern Scree, both wearing their necklaces of bones,
led Heep forth. Heep kept his yellow eyes lowered, but
Faolan could see the smile on his muzzle.

A drizzle had started and was quickly turning the
dust into a fine, slippery mud. Heep stepped forward to
deliver the gnaw bite. The yellow wolf would tear a piece
from Faolan's pelt and possibly his flesh. Faolan would be
marked by Heep, cut right to his bone if the bite was deep
enough. The idea was appalling to him.

Faolan stared at the ground, not daring to look up. His heart was beating so hard in his chest, it seemed as loud as Thunderheart's. Indeed, it was as if thunder rolled through him. He pawed the ground nervously with his splayed foot. Faolan could smell Heep's hot breath as he stepped closer. He would not give Heep the satisfaction of running or even flinching. He braced himself for the first tearing of his flesh. *I must not waver. I must stand here. I will do this, for Thunderheart.* And it was as if the great grizzly's heart invaded him, not simply the booming sound, but the lifeblood pumping through him. Faolan shifted slightly and planted his feet, prepared to endure the pain of the bite.

He was not sure how long he had stood when he noticed a silence had fallen on the wolves gathered around. What was happening? Nothing. What was wrong? He could feel the other wolves shrinking back in disappointment, as if the drama they had anticipated was fading. He lifted his eyes and saw Heep quivering with fear, those two yellow eyes riveted on the print Faolan's splayed forepaw had made in the mud. It was a perfect spiral like that of a swirling star. Faolan blinked. He had never left such a deep track before, and the spiraling lines on the pad of his paw were so dim that they had never left a trace. Had he pressed that hard in his determination not to move? But why was Heep quivering? Everything was turned around. Faolan was supposed to be the one trembling in fear.

"Get on with it, lad!" Lord Claren gave Heep a cuff.

"Oh, Lord Claren," Heep said as he sank to his knees and began to screw his face into the mud, carefully avoiding the paw print. "I am not worthy of this honor. Thank you. It is very kind of you to offer. There are wolves enough to tread on me in my lowly rankless condition. That I should bite this wolf without doing outrage to the other gnaw wolves' feelings is … is … is …"

"Is what, by Lupus?" The lord of the pack leaped upon Heep's quaking head and slammed it farther into the mud. Snarling, he made a grab for Heep's face and violently shook his muzzle for several seconds before finally flinging him away.

Faolan was mystified. He was the one supposed to be bitten, and yet Heep's blood scrawled the air like a tracer of red lightning while Faolan stood unbloodied and unbowed. He quickly corrected his erect posture as Lord Claren approached with Lord Bhreac. Faolan arched his back and started the first of his submission postures. He quickly sank onto his knees, but before he could even begin to roll over to expose his belly, both lords slammed on top of him and clamped him firmly to the ground with their forepaws.

The weight of the two wolves was crushing, and once again, Faolan braced himself for a mauling. He could barely breathe. He heard the lords begin to talk in low whispers. "Positively unspeakable," Lord Claren said.

"Yes, but that is just the point. That's why he must be taken immediately to the Carreg Gaer so the chieftain can talk to him."

"But the chieftain is dying! The *raghnaid* can deal with this gnaw wolf later. There is no rush."

"He must go while the chieftain still lives."

Something within Faolan wilted. Although he was nearly numb from the crushing weight of the two lords, he could still feel shame. Duncan MacDuncan had treated him with patience and respect when Faolan had jumped the wall of fire. To face the chieftain again, disgraced, would be worse than any gnaw bite.

CHAPTER FIVE

THE LAST WORDS
OF A CHIEFTAIN

THE CAMP OF THE CARREG GAER
was smaller than Faolan had anticipated but situated in a
region of lovely soaring cliffs with a creek running right
through the middle. Some young pups were chasing one
another across the shallows, their hind paws furiously
splashing up water and flinging mud.

Along the banks, elder wolves were playing a game
called *biliboo* with pebbles from the creek and knuckle-
bones. The game was one of strategy and required great
mental concentration. Played by four wolves in teams of
two, the pieces were moved from one side of a complicated pattern scratched in the dirt to another. The paths
through which they moved were intricate and governed
by a rigid set of rules. Faolan had often tried to watch in
his own pack and understand the intricacies of the moves.

The players never spoke a word during the game, and it seemed as if their pieces flowed across the pattern, almost as if they were never even touched by the wolves' muzzles or paws.

Faolan had been told to wait by a red-speckled rock to be called into the cave for the *raghnaid*. He looked up into the star-powdered night, searching for signs of the new constellations that appeared during the Caribou Moon. He found great comfort in searching the sky, hunting for the old familiar constellations that had sailed through the nights in the seasons he had spent with Thunderheart.

It seemed colder than normal for this moon, and he wondered if the creek the pups were playing in would be frozen by morning. But there were not even glimpses of the first stars of the snow moons yet. *Curious*, he thought. He scanned the sky for other constellations. Faolan especially liked the star picture that the grizzly bears called the Great Claws. Thunderheart had told him that the owls called it the Golden Talons, and he'd learned that the wolves called it the Great Fangs. But the constellation was almost gone now and would not return until early winter. Other constellations had begun to rise. That of the caribou would climb higher and higher following the horns of the Caribou Moon during the frosty autumn evenings, and soon the caribou's mate and calf would walk behind him across the night. Faolan missed the Great Claws. He didn't even like the wolf name for the constellation. The Great Fangs—how stupid! It made him think of slobber in the skies, long threads of saliva spinning off into the night just like Mhairie running with the *byrrgis*.

Talk about a temper! He had never experienced such a drubbing. It was so different from the usual abuse. That slobbering mouth never quit! Although she had not slobbered when she stood over him, yelling her head off.

He looked up again, searching for the Great Claws, which would always remind him of Thunderheart.

When he glanced away from the stars, he saw a thin, white wolf looking at him as she passed by the rock where he waited. His blood froze. He got up to move away but still felt her eyes on him. There was no mistaking who this wolf was. Lael, the clan's new Obea. The Obea was the female wolf in each clan responsible for removing deformed pups from the whelping den, tearing them from their mother's milk to take them to a *tummfraw*, a place of abandonment where the pup would die. If the she-wolf he had seen with Lord Bhreac and Lord Claren delivered a *malcadh*, it would be Lael who would carry it away. Unless, of course, the mother went *by-lang* and succeeded in losing herself and the pup in the deep away. Faolan felt the green eyes of the white wolf following him.

A pup now ran up to where he was waiting.

"You're big for a gnaw wolf," the pup said. "I mean you're big for any wolf."

"Yeah," said another.

"He's bigger than my da."

"My da and my mum put together!" said another.

"Hey! He should be doing a submission roll."

"But he's so big," whispered a rust-colored wolf.

"Doesn't matter, he's a gnaw wolf." The other pup came forward. She, too, was rust colored and must have been his sister.

"You're supposed to get down, you know. I mean, you're already in trouble."

"Yes, yes, I know. Sorry." Faolan began to sink to his knees.

"You talk funny, too," said the bossy little wolf.

"My mum says he talks like a bear." A new pup had now come up to watch the spectacle by the red rock.

"A grizzly bear was my second Milk Giver," Faolan

said, twisting his neck so his face pushed into the ground. *I cannot believe I am doing this. I am five times the size of these pups.*

"A bear. Weird! What was it like?" the first pup asked. He was a genuinely curious little fellow and had crouched down a bit to get on eye level with Faolan.

"Are you scared of going in to see the *raghnaid*?" asked a gray female pup.

"Are you *cag mag*? If a bear was his Milk Giver, you think he's scared of the *raghnaid*?" said the curious pup, who was still crouching.

But they were wrong. Faolan was scared, not of the *raghnaid* so much but of the shame of facing Duncan MacDuncan.

The half dozen or so pups who had crept out from behind the red rock soon became bored and went off to wrestle on a patch of scoured ground. Faolan looked across at them. Two other pups had escaped from their parents' den and were trying to nose their way into the tussle, but their mother came out, gave them each a swat that sent them flying, and then growled. The pups obediently followed her back into their den.

A shaft of moonlight suddenly poured down and illuminated another she-wolf and her two pups. Their coats were a silvery gray, much like Faolan's own, and Faolan tried to imagine what his life might have been like if his paw had been straight and not splayed. If he'd had a wolf mother and father or sisters and brothers to play with in the moonlight, to cuff him soundly on the muzzle and make him follow them back into a cozy den. He would have known then that the Great Claws were called the Great Fangs.

Faolan groaned and sank down to his knees, but he would not screw his face into the dirt even though he saw a high-ranking male wolf stride toward him. He rolled to one side and looked at the stars. There was a swirl of clouds that thinly veiled the moon. The clouds quickly scudded away, but for just a moment, they looked identical to the whirl of lines on the pad of his splayed paw. Why had that upset the yellow wolf Heep so much? Heep had backed off from biting him because he was frightened. And yet the first time Faolan had ever looked at those swirled markings, he had found them deeply comforting. He had thought the whirling tracery spoke of something marvelous, hinted that he was part of a larger pattern of endlessly spiraling harmony.

At that moment, Faolan's reveries were interrupted.

"Up, gnaw wolf," a pack elder growled. "Duncan MacDuncan is ready to see you. Mind you do the proper veneration and obeisance as you approach. The chieftain is failing rapidly and it is most important that submission rituals be upheld. None of your blasphemous *byrrgis* behavior, cur. Are you ready?"

"Yes," Faolan said meekly, and rose to follow the pack elder. He was careful to tuck his tail between his legs and lay his ears flat despite having a terrible itch in one that seemed to bother him more, the flatter he laid his ears.

The chieftain's cave was immense, and in the center was a pit with a fire burning in it. On the wall hung scraped hides and an array of antlers—deer, caribou, musk ox—all of which had the most intricate carvings. Faolan tried to keep his gaze down, but it seemed his eyes were drawn back to the flames.

The clan elders who comprised the *raghnaid* were in their ceremonial headdresses of gnawed bones and necklaces, and it seemed to Faolan that there were only two sounds in the cave—the crackling and snapping of the fire as it devoured the air, and the odd clicking rattle of bones. No one spoke. But when Faolan glanced up, he saw something he had not expected in their eyes—fear. *Do they really think I am moon rot?* he wondered.

The ancient wolf Duncan MacDuncan was reclining on the pelt of a bull elk. Once he had been a wolf with a dark gray coat, but with age, he was almost white. There were bare patches on his shoulders that revealed scars from long-ago combat. His shoulders almost suggested a landscape of the battlefields he had known. Like scorched earth, it was as if the fur had refused to grow there any longer. His eyes were milky green, the color of the streams that ran down from the glaciers in the high country. There was a notch in one of his ears, and it was not hard to imagine the cougar who had torn it.

Behind him, soaring into the shadows, were two racks of the most enormous caribou antlers Faolan had ever seen. Beside the chief an elegant she-wolf rested on her haunches, her head held high. It was Cathmor, the chieftain's mate. Her dark gray coat was almost black, and her eyes a lovely shade of green that reminded Faolan of the mossed rocks in the river where he and Thunderheart had fished their only summer together.

"Bring him forth," the chieftain wheezed. The elder who had escorted Faolan gave him a rough nudge, and

Faolan began the traditional belly crawl toward the pelt where Duncan MacDuncan lay. The sight of this once noble chieftain shocked Faolan. Duncan MacDuncan looked broken, as if the slightest blow would shatter him completely.

"Close enough," the elder said after a few seconds.

"No! Closer," Duncan MacDuncan rasped.

When Faolan reached the edge of the pelt, he twisted his neck and began to grind his face into the floor. He caught a glimpse of the fire out of the corner of one eye. His hackles started to rise and then settled, and a calm stole through him.

The chieftain stirred slightly on his pelt. "Easy, my dear heart," Cathmor whispered, and lay a calming paw on the chieftain's flank.

What has this lad seen in the flames? the chieftain wondered. *Does he see that it is about to snow before the snow moons? That this spring, the ice will not crack until it is almost the Moon of the Singing Grass? Is the time of the Long Cold returning?*

If Faolan has the fire sight, then indeed he is a special wolf, thought Duncan MacDuncan, *and a portent of grievous times ahead.* Then the chieftain shook his head as if to clear it of such dire thoughts. He had a last duty to perform. As supreme leader of the clan and high lord of the *raghnaid*, he opened the proceedings.

"Faolan, gnaw wolf of the MacDuncan clan, the *raghnaid* has been assembled to determine if your actions during a recent *byrrgis* constitute a violation of our laws. Nearly one thousand years ago, when our ancestors were led here by the first Fengo, we planted laws, traditions, and codes of behavior as thickly as the trees of the deep forests from whence we came. Because we believed that a country without laws was more dangerous than one without trees, that without them, dignified and noble wolves could not stand upright in the fierce winds that sweep our land."

The chieftain then turned to Lord Adair, second highest lord of the *raghnaid*, and called, "Read the charges."

Lord Adair came forward with a bone and began to read: "As recorded by the gnaw wolf, Heep, of the River Pack of the MacDuncan clan. On the morning after the fifteenth night of the Caribou Moon, a *byrrgis* was assembled on the Burn in pursuit of a bull moose. In the first quarter of the hunt, at press-paw speed, the gnaw wolf Faolan followed meticulously his obligations of sniffing and reporting on the droppings."

You bet I did, thought Faolan, as if Heep were right there reading the bone himself. *You idiot wolf who wanted to go in my place with your dry nose and not a trace of dung to report on it!*

"I humbly pursued my course on the western flank, a flank much too grand for my base origins. As diligently as possible, I searched out urine pools of the moose and, in my most humble opinion, was able to confirm that the beast was healthy. It was not until press-paw speed had broken into attack speed that I noticed a disturbance that seemed to flow through the *byrrgis*, reaching back as far as my lowly position as a sweeper. It was at that time that I looked up and saw the gnaw wolf Faolan streaking through the *byrrgis* and cutting out to overtake the young and noble outflanker Mhairie, who, due to her outstanding abilities, had been sent from the Carreg Gaer of the MacDuncans. At the moment he overtook her, chaos began to erode the *hwlyn* of the *byrrgis*."

There was a gasp from the other members of the *raghnaid*. *Hwlyn* was the wolf word meaning "spirit of the pack." Exclamations of shock and horror swirled through the *gadderheal*. Tails that seconds before were hanging loosely suddenly tucked nearly as tightly as Faolan's, not in submission but in fear.

"Continue," Duncan MacDuncan ordered calmly. The wolf Adair read on, concluding with a description of how Faolan had risen on his hind legs, and the bull moose had wheeled about in a panic to charge the *byrrgis*, "thus cleaving the spirit of the pack."

"Was any wolf killed or injured by the moose when it charged?" Duncan MacDuncan asked with renewed vigor.

"No, sir," replied Adair.

"Then I say that is rather a ... well ... promiscuous use of the word 'cleave.'" Again a shudder passed through the *gadderheal*. For a wolf who was so close to death himself to use the wolf word for dying so calmly was unnerving, if not to the chieftain at least to the others in the ceremonial cave. "What's this gnaw wolf's name? The one who gnawed this bone?"

"Heep, my lord."

"Aaah, Heep, yes, Heep, the one who is always carrying on about being humble. Bring the bone to my pelt so I might examine it."

The wolf Adair stepped forward and dropped the bone. It rested in the thick pelt of the bull elk inches from Faolan's muzzle. He had seen a few bones that Heep had gnawed, and once more, Faolan noticed the subtle scratches made by Heep's flawed rear-slicing tooth. Either the nick in that tooth had deepened or Heep had been more careless than usual in his work, because it was quite visible on this gnaw-bone.

"So what do you think, lad?" Duncan MacDuncan's breath was hot and slightly fetid. It was the breath of a sick wolf. He spoke low and tapped his tail as a signal that the others were to back away. He wanted a private conversation.

"Me? What do I think?" Faolan asked. He shoved his ears forward with new alertness. His tail lifted a very tiny bit. He hadn't been asked what he thought about anything since he had arrived in the Beyond.

"Yes, what do you think about the gnaw-bone?"

He looked up at the chieftain. Duncan MacDuncan's eyes were a rheumy green. His muzzle twist was unkempt. Only clan chieftains and members of the Watch were permitted to wear the twisted braid. "Well, my lord, I am sorry to say every scratch, every mark the gnaw wolf Heep carved is true. I violated the order. I am deeply sorry."

"Oh, I know that, and I'm glad to hear you're sorry. But what do you think of the workmanship, the craft?"

Faolan was shocked. He slid his eyes up and gazed into the faded ones of the old chieftain. Was a lowly gnaw wolf like himself really permitted to comment on any-thing, let alone another gnaw wolf's ability?

"I . . . I . . ." Faolan stammered.

"Now, for Lupus' sake, don't say the word 'humble.' Just give your opinion, lad."

"I don't think it's that good, my lord. He carves too deep for one thing, and every line is the same—the same depth, the same width."

"Hmmm" was all the old chieftain said. He sighed and then commenced a racking cough. Cathmor came up to him and began licking his muzzle and lightly stroking his fur with her paw.

"What am I supposed to do with you, lad?" the chief-tain whispered hoarsely.

"I don't know, my lord. I am not a very good gnaw wolf."

"No! No! That's not the problem at all. You're a frinking good gnaw wolf." Faolan was not sure exactly what "frinking" meant, but he thought it was one of the minor curse words that was shared with the owls, for Gwynneth had used it several times. "But you're a pathetic pack wolf. You don't understand, do you? This whole pack, clan business."

"I guess not, my lord."

"Guess not? I *know* not. There is no guessing about it."

"So I must leave."

"Why?"

"Because I'm not a good pack wolf. I guess I'm just a lone wolf."

"That's not your privilege. I do the saying around here!" Duncan MacDuncan roared. It was as if a current went through the cave, and every filament of fur on every wolf's hackles suddenly stood straight up.

In a low, hoarse whisper, Duncan asked Faolan, "Do you know what a *gaddergnaw* is?"

Faolan shook his head.

"We have not had one in several years. It's a contest to select a gnaw wolf—the best gnaw wolf—for the Watch at the Ring of Sacred Volcanoes. It will be a hard contest, lad. They choose one wolf, and on rare occasions two, and never two from the same clan. So it makes the competition all the harder for you. And for Heep." He paused. "You have it in you, Faolan."

Duncan studied Faolan carefully as if he were looking for the wolf that might lurk inside, as if in the bright green light of this young wolf's eyes he might see the reflection of a traveling wolf from another time. "You could be selected. You have fine teeth for carving and you have strength. However, you have no sense. But the *gad-dergnaw*, Faolan—this could be your chance!"

MacDuncan now staggered to his feet and, lifting his tail painfully, wagged it once, twice, then a third time to summon the other wolves closer.

"The gnaw-bone has been read. There is clear evidence that the gnaw wolf Faolan is guilty of a most serious infraction of the *gaddernock* code as it is applied to the *byrrgis*. He has challenged the order. He has admitted his guilt as well as his profound regret. From my private conversation with him, I can say that he knows deep in his marrow that he can do better, that he can become a clan wolf."

What private conversation was this? When did I ever say that? Faolan wondered.

"And so," the chieftain continued, "from the time of the Ice March, I invoke the privilege of the Sayer. I say that this gnaw wolf shall stay in the clan. He shall resume his lowly position as gnaw wolf in the Pack of the Eastern Scree. He shall be required to visit every outflanker of every pack of the MacDuncan clan, present this bone gnawed by Heep, and perform the third-degree submission and veneration rituals, as dictated by section thirty-two of the *byrrgnock* code of the *gaddernock*. Following the contrition rituals, he shall gnaw a bone of contrition to be left with the pack outflankers. Thus shall he gain absolution."

Duncan paused now, his legs trembling with fatigue from standing, his chest heaving from speaking. His mate, Cathmor, touched his flank. "Please, dear, rest."

He growled, "Rest! There is eternity for resting! I have one more announcement I have to make—an important one. I have received a message from Finbar Fengo of the Watch. We have agreed that another *gaddergnaw* must be held."

A murmur of excitement swept through the wolves. Tails began to wag. It had been years since the last *gaddergnaw*.

"All the clans shall gather here in the Moon of the Singing Grass. This is what I, Duncan MacDuncan, chieftain of the clan of the MacDuncans, say."

And let us hope, Duncan thought to himself, *that indeed the grass will be singing and not still locked under frozen ground.* His eyes were more filmy than before, and a terrible rattling wheeze shook his frail body. He sank onto the pelts, weak from his efforts.

A hush filled the cave. It was very rare that a chieftain invoked the privilege of the Sayer. But Duncan

MacDuncan just had, and the word of a dying chieftain carried great weight.

As Faolan was led away from the chieftain, he took one more glance at the fire. He blinked and hesitated. In the flames, he spied a pattern that was familiar—a swirl of bright orange and yellow buried deep at the base of the smaller flames hovering just above the coal bed.

I see it—the same spiral that marks my paw. By my marrow, I see it in the fire of the gadderheal!

CHAPTER SIX

MHAIRIE'S DEN

MHAIRIE SLID DOWN THE SHORT
steep tunnel to her den. She was so happy to have her
own private space. The new litter of pups that her mum,
Caila, had delivered four months before had made everything so crowded. So she and her sister Dearlea took turns
living in this solitary den while the other helped Caila
tend the new ones.

The pups were at that most difficult age. Old enough
to get into trouble but not old enough to get out of it.
They were fascinated—as all young pups were—by the
tantalizing whiteness at the mouth of their den. They
thought the white light that flooded the opening was a
wall and not simply the light of day. Mhairie wondered if
she had felt that way when she was their age. But she
could hardly remember.

Caila had chosen a whelping den with an especially long tunnel. "Keep them from the light as long as possible," she said to her mate, Eiric. "I can't go chasing after them if they get out, and you know they always try as soon as their milk teeth come in."

Sure enough, when their milk teeth broke in, chaos broke out! Especially with six! The worst part was their howling. Mhairie wasn't sure why, but wolf pup cries were nothing like the melodious howls of mature wolves. For at least six moons, their howls were sharp barks, like the clash of hard rocks tumbling against one another in a slide. When the earthquake of the previous winter had struck, at first it sounded to her like ten thousand pups storming out of their whelping dens. And then there were the pups' whiny whimpers when they begged. Not as loud as barks, but annoyingly squeaky.

Mhairie wondered if she would ever be able to be a good mother. It was so exhausting. *How does Mum stand it?* she wondered. But Caila did. And who would have thought that Caila would give birth to six lively pups at her advanced age? Not a *malcadh* among them.

But now Mhairie felt a terrible loneliness and anger. Why had that gnaw wolf gone and spoiled everything for her? When she came back, the wolves, the outflankers in the MacDuncan clan who had sent her to run with this *byrrgis*, were visibly disappointed. Alastrine, the point wolf of the chieftain's pack, tried to soothe Mhairie in her thick musical brogue, for she was also the *skreeleen* of the pack. She delighted in using the old wolf phrases that had come with the wolves on the Ice March from the Long Cold more than a thousand years earlier. "Don't worry, my dear heart. Don't *greet*." *Greet* was an old wolf word, which meant "to fret." "You're so young. Younger than I ever was when I ran with the outflankers. Another day, another hunt, another *byrrgis*, dearie. Be patient."

He wrecked everything was all Mhairie could think. *That moldwarp, beslubbering, canker-livered gnaw wolf.* She dredged up from her brain every vile wolf curse she could think of and was muttering them into the darkness of her den. These were words that would have earned her a muzzle-flinging nip from her mum. She could almost feel Caila's jaws clamping down on her and hurling her across the cave.

But it wasn't just that Faolan had demolished her first-ever run with the outflankers. There was more to it, and she was almost as angry with herself as with the gnaw wolf. What was it about this wolf that had gotten under her pelt like a summer tick and annoyed her almost as much as her younger brothers and sisters? And yet, just as with her younger pup siblings, she felt a need to look out for Faolan. Or to beat him like the wrath of Lupus and turn his bones to dust!

CHAPTER SEVEN

THE PAW OF
THUNDERHEART

FAOLAN SET OFF IMMEDIATELY
after being escorted from the *gadderheal*. Adair had led
him to the edge of the Carreg Gaer's territory and had
given him directions for finding the other packs of the
MacDuncan clan, as well as instructions in the rituals of
contrition. Faolan listened, but his mind was occupied
with something else. The words of Duncan MacDuncan
echoed in his ears.

Do you know what a gaddergnaw *is? . . . a contest to
select a gnaw wolf—the best gnaw wolf—for the Watch
at the Ring of Sacred Volcanoes. . . . You have it in you,
Faolan. . . . You could be selected. You have fine teeth
for carving and you have strength. However, you have no
sense. But the* gaddergnaw, *Faolan—this could be your
chance!*

A high-ranking wolf sending off a shamed gnaw wolf normally would have given him a sharp, almost stunning blow to the top of his muzzle, but the slap that Adair administered qualified somewhere between a pat and a thwack. Indeed, it almost missed Faolan's muzzle entirely, for Adair could not bear to look at Faolan. *He sees moon rot in me, but Duncan MacDuncan didn't. Duncan MacDuncan saw something else!*

"Be on your way, gnaw wolf," Adair snarled. "Learn from your disgrace! Roll in the scent of your shame. And save any dreams you might entertain of the *gadder-gnaw*. For while you are on your trail of shame, the gnaw wolves' preparation for the competition will begin in earnest." He paused, then added nastily, "And you shall miss out!"

And so Faolan set off into the darkness with his bone of shame gripped in his mouth.

There is a time of night when the world seems almost empty. There is an overwhelming hollowness after the moon has slipped away to another world, and the constellations have slid to another Beyond. The stars expire one by one like the last small breaths of illumination in the darkness, and the night goes dead before the first weak glow of the dawn.

Faolan had not traveled far before Alastrine's first howls scored the night. He stopped in his tracks. So the chieftain had passed. A shiver went through Faolan from his raised hackles to his tail, still firmly tucked between his legs. He fell to his knees and put his paws over his muzzle. This was the first true act of humility that Faolan had made since he had been with the wolves.

Soon braided through the howls of the *skreeleen* was the fine filament of Cathmor's voice keening the loss of her mate. *What a terrible time to die,* thought Faolan. For during these emptiest hours in the hollow of the night, there was not a sign of the star ladder to the heavenly constellation that the wolves called the Cave of Souls. Those stars had slipped away to the west already and in a few nights would disappear entirely for the three winter moons that would soon be upon the wolves of the Beyond. For those few remaining nights, Cathmor howled her thanks. Had it been the time of the winter moons, Duncan MacDuncan's soul would have had to wait until spring to climb the star ladder and enter the Cave of Souls.

The *skreeleen's* pitch changed to howl the summoning, calling all the MacDuncan packs to head to the far west, where the night was still young and the star ladder could be found. They were to travel at triple press-paw speed to catch it. For the next three nights, the wolves would gather there to howl the *morriah*, the lament for their dead chieftain. Gnaw wolves were excluded from this ceremony. Therefore, Faolan's charge to visit all of the packs and perform his rituals of contrition would be delayed. He had wanted only to get it over with, but Duncan MacDuncan was the one wolf that Faolan had truly admired. In his marrow, he felt a keenness for the old chieftain that he had never come close to feeling for any other creature except Thunderheart.

Thunderheart! The name exploded in Faolan's mind. He had not been to the place where he had buried her paw since he had joined the MacDuncan clan. To touch the bone of the paw that had cradled him was now what Faolan wanted most in the world. Just being near that bone would give him comfort.

He veered sharply south and headed toward the river from which Thunderheart had rescued him. She'd told him that the word *fao* meant both "river" and "wolf." *Lan* meant "gift." And when she had dredged him up from the swollen turbulence of the river, she had thought of him as the river's gift to her. She had just lost her own cub to a cougar, and her milk was still running. So she became Faolan's milk mother, and nourished him. When Thunderheart died, Faolan had taken the largest bone from his milk mother's paw and carved on it the story of their golden summer together, of swimming behind schools of trout and standing in the rapids at the time of the salmon spawn and scooping fish from the roiling waters. It was all there on the bone. The kill of their first caribou, the summer den, the winter den. He had buried the bone on a shale slope of a high ridge near the salt lagoons. It was a spot a fair distance from any of the wolf packs. Faolan had not wanted any wolf to see the bone he had carved. It was his story, his memory, and to him it was sacred. The wolves had a code, a law, a rule for everything. This was Faolan's code. *And by my marrow,* he thought, *it is right!*

He arrived just as the first thin, red slash of dawn light bled above the horizon. The sun rose, then faded to pink and dissolved into the flawless blue sky of morning. It did not take Faolan long to find his bone. When he heard the first click of his dewclaw against the bone, he began to dig delicately with his mouth, sheathing his teeth, and finally using just his tongue to lift the bone from the earth. He licked off the dust, and his eyes filled as he saw the markings on the bone that told the story of what had been his life. He swung his head from the paw of Thunderheart to the bone of shame that Heep had carved. He wanted to fling that horrid bone of shame into the deepest part of the river, throw it into a fire, throw it straight down to the Dim World. But he felt a calm steal over him suddenly. It was as if a phantom paw stroked the fur just beneath his jaws, the most sensitive region on any wolf.

Faolan licked the paw bone, and his finely etched lines stood in beautiful relief against its whiteness. He felt almost outside his own skin, his own pelt, hovering just above himself. He watched himself swim just behind Thunderheart in search of fish, then saw a tiny pup who was supposed to be digging for roots and bulbs begin nosing instead at a small hill of sandy dirt. Seconds later, the cub had uncovered an ant's nest and was yowling his head off. His muzzle was stinging ferociously. Thunderheart raced toward him and scraped off the nasty creatures with her own rough tongue. He would welcome back the stinging fury of those ants if

it meant he could be with Thunderheart and feel the
rasp of her tongue, hear the thunderous beating of her
great heart.

O Thunderheart, I long to see you,
feel your booming heart in my blood.
O Thunderheart, you're always with me,
though far away beyond the river
in the stars of Ursulana.
O Thunderheart, I'll seek you always,
when my time comes.
In a night long away
we'll meet in the heavens of wolf or bear.
By my marrow I shall find you there
no matter where you may wander.
I am your pup, your cub, forever!

And though he sang to Thunderheart, all the while
he also thought of Duncan MacDuncan, the wolf who
had told him he had no sense but did have a chance—a
chance to be a better wolf.

Later, as night fell far from where the lone wolf keened
his song for his milk mother, the chieftain's mate,

Cathmor, wailed her grief into the northern wind. On this the second night of the *morriah*, she saw a luminous gray mist at the very top of the star ladder of the spirit trail that led to the Cave of Souls.

"The *lochin! Lochin!*" she called. She knew in her marrow that there was now a gulf between her and the luminous spirit of her mate as deep as any sea, as wide as the distance between the earth and any star. But she would look for that mist every evening as the iridescent spheres of dew drifted down through the pearly light of the moon. The *lochin* was how the spirits of the dead lived on in the hearts of the ones they had left behind, making their marrow tingle until the time when they, too, climbed the star ladder to the Cave of Souls.

CHAPTER EIGHT

THE TRAIL
OF SHAME

THE MACDUNCAN CLAN WAS comprised of five packs of wolves. Faolan had already performed the ritual of contrition at the pack of the Carreg Gaer in front of Elpeth, Stellan, and Mhairie, the outflankers. But there were three other packs he must visit with the bone of shame before returning to his own. They were the River Pack, the Pack of the Blue Rock, and the Pack of the Fire Grass. The Blue Rock Pack was on the border with MacDuff territory. It would be a whole day's run at half press-paw from where he was, and then if he started early the next day, he would be able to travel west to the River Pack. Faolan really wanted to get that over with fast, for he could just imagine Heep's pleasure in seeing Faolan having to grovel with the bone of shame in his mouth.

Faolan had been thinking all this as he traveled the trail of shame. Soon in the long blue dusk, a raggedy wolf trotted out toward him. The wolf made a strange noise that was neither a bark nor a howl but a kind of strangled whistling. Faolan knew instantly that it must be the gnaw wolf from the Blue Rock Pack. He had heard about this wolf who had been born with a crookedness deep in his throat that made his every utterance sound like a whistle. Thus his nickname, the Whistler.

The only time a gnaw wolf was expected to show submission to another gnaw wolf was on the trail of shame. Faolan immediately prostrated himself before the Whistler, a pale gray wolf who seemed painfully thin.

"I did not expect to arrive so quickly. I didn't know I was so close to the honorable Blue Rock Pack," Faolan said after dropping the bone from his mouth.

"You aren't. I was just out hoping for a hare. They are often where the lichen eaters graze and much easier prey."

"I've heard about lichen eaters but never seen one," Faolan replied. "Their meat is supposed to be very tasty." He knew they had antlers and appeared nearly identical to caribou but were smaller and seemed to have a taste for lichen as much as for the grasses that caribou fed on. The Whistler definitely needed easy prey, from the looks of his bones, which appeared to be nearly jutting through his pelt.

"You can rise up now," the Whistler said.

"Are you sure?" Faolan was trying to do everything just right. He would become the best possible gnaw wolf he could, so he could leave the clans behind and beome a member of the Watch.

"Yes, please come. They are expecting you."

Faolan was taken aback. No wolf had said "please" to him since he had been taken into the clan. He tucked the bone snugly under his chin and began to walk. But then he stopped. This poor wolf looked as if he hadn't had a decent meal in months.

"What's the problem?" The Whistler turned around.

"Why don't we go track down some of those lichen eaters. I've never hunted them. And you look as if you could use a good meal."

The Whistler twitched his ears. "You know how it is in a big pack like the Blue Rock. I'm last to eat after twenty-five others."

"Twenty-five! How do you get even a bite?"

"Often I don't." He sighed. "I mostly go after hare. Small stuff. Not very satisfying. No fat on a hare, you know."

"I know. So let's go after these lichen eaters. There's time. You said I'm early."

"Are you sure? I mean, you think just the two of us could do it? Take down a lichen eater?"

"Well, if we succeed, it's going to be a lot tastier than a hare. And two have a better chance than one," Faolan answered.

"I certainly could use some real meat. I think we might be able to pick up a trail yonder." He nodded toward a dry creek bed. "They often travel through that way."

"Let's go," Faolan said.

They found the trail immediately.

"One of them might be limping," the Whistler said after a few minutes. "It's setting down its east foreleg unevenly."

Faolan was impressed. The Whistler was clearly an observant wolf and knew how to read tracks.

It was hardly a herd, just four lichen eaters traveling together, two females, a calf, and an elderly male.

The male had a deep wound in its hock and was indeed limping. It seemed to Faolan as if he would be an easy takedown. The strategy was simple. Split the male off from the others and chase him down. Faolan and the Whistler were working well together and gaining on the old male by playing a bluff strategy in which they would run him hard for a period, then ease up and feign loss of interest. This gave the prey a sense of false security so that it became less vigilant, perhaps even stopped to take a rest. Faolan had the feeling that this was just about to happen, when all of a sudden, they heard a commotion in the brush on a hillside. A big healthy buck came charging down a slope, stopped a short distance from them, and pawed the ground. Lichen eaters were generally fleet and small of build, but this one was huge. There was nothing small about him. The buck began dipping and raising his immense rack of antlers. Faolan had seen caribou do this. It was an aggression display that often preceded territorial conflicts or mating battles among male members of a herd. But he had never seen it used in confrontation with predators.

"Uh-oh!" the Whistler groaned. "We better get out of here!" But Faolan wheeled about, dug in his four paws, shoved his ears forward, and snarled at the buck, who was lowering his head as if to charge.

What is this wolf doing? the Whistler thought.

There was a silver streak, like a low-flying comet in the twilight.

It took the Whistler a moment to figure out that the streak was Faolan hurling through the air. There was a large smack and an expulsion of breath, followed by a high whinnying screech. Faolan was straddling the shoulders of the buck, who reared into the air. The buck took off like a bolt, but Faolan clung, with the Whistler following.

It was absolutely the strangest thing the Whistler had ever seen. He had been there when Faolan vaulted over the wall of fire set up to trap him. The Whistler knew how the descriptions were soon exaggerated, and it was not long before Faolan was said to have jumped for the sun. But there was no exaggeration needed for what the Whistler was witnessing here. Faolan was actually riding a buck lichen eater, blood flying in their wake.

The blood was the buck's. Faolan had sunk his long fangs into the buck's neck and pierced the life-giving artery. His claws were embedded so deeply in one shoulder that the buck's muscles were torn. The lichen eater began to stumble, then soon crumpled to the ground. The buck's stomach was heaving, and his chest worked to draw every breath. The Whistler came up, and both he and Faolan sank to their knees, laying their heads close to the dying buck's and peering into his eyes, searching for that last guttering of light. The death ritual of *lochinvyrr* was not code, nor law engraved on any bone. It was an urge that flowed stronger than hunger through a wolf, a need to let the dying animal know that the life it gave was valued.

For several seconds, Faolan and the Whistler were silent, their thoughts focused on the beauty of this animal's grace and spirit. *You are worthy, your life is worthy, your meat will sustain us.* There was a moment just before the last beat of the animal's heart when a light flickered deep in its eyes, as if an agreement had come to pass. A second later, the buck died.

Thin, frayed clouds floated low over the darkening horizon like cobwebs clinging to the day. Faolan and the Whistler ate for a long time, until the moon began to rise in the eastern sky, and then, with heavy bellies, they turned toward the Pack of the Blue Rock.

Faolan was supposed to follow behind the Whistler, but they soon fell into a companionable trot shoulder to shoulder. It seemed natural to Faolan, and he had hardly been aware of it until the Whistler spoke.

"I was there when you jumped the wall of fire." The words came like a wind rising up from the depths of a deep canyon. "I was one of the wolves who chased you there. And now you are the one who has given me my first decent food in weeks." He paused. "Thank you."

There was a long silence. This was the first wolf who had admitted to being a part of the *byrrgis* that had tried to drive Faolan to his death when they thought he had the foaming-mouth disease. He didn't think that any of them had felt guilty about mistaking him for a foaming-mouth wolf. What had disturbed them was that Faolan had not died. Instead, he had jumped the wall of fire meant to catch him, jumping for the sun and challenging the order of the Great Chain. This was considered a blasphemous act, not to be spoken of again but consigned to the silence of a carved bone. To talk about it casually, or "off the bone" as the Whistler was doing, was not acceptable.

"You'd better not talk about it," Faolan said.

The Whistler shrugged and then, with a strange

chuckle that sounded like a rattling wind, said, "I don't exactly speak, now, do I? Would you consider this a voice?"

Well, Faolan thought, *they are words, even if they sound odd.* "Can I ask you about the *gaddergnaw?*"

"I know very little. There hasn't been one since I've been with the Blue Rock Pack." The Whistler paused. "However, they do say that during the competition, they treat the gnaw wolves with great respect. No cuffing, no muzzle bites. None of that nonsense."

"And after the *gaddergnaw?*"

"Well, I'm afraid, for all but the one wolf selected, it's life as usual."

Life as usual! These were bitter, bitter words. Faolan simply had to be selected, and yet he already felt far behind.

"Have you started the practice yet?"

"Oh, yes, one of the *gadderlords,* the wolves who run the competition, came and prepared me for the type of bones we shall be asked to carve."

"What type is that?"

"The usual. More inscriptions of the Great Chain — no surprise there! And then, a bone of our own making."

"What do you mean?"

"A story bone. That, I think, will be the most diffi-cult. When we all traveled to the west country to perform the mourning ceremonies for the great chieftain of the MacDuncan clan, they had us practice on some bones. We carved grieving bones for Duncan MacDuncan, and the lords came around and told us what was good and what wasn't in our carving."

Faolan couldn't help but think how far behind he must be without the benefit of this early training.

"And then there is a *byrrgis* in which we are not sweepers." The Whistler nodded at Faolan. "You'll do well."

Faolan dropped his head. "I hope so," he mumbled.

"I know so. You're built for it."

They came up on the pack's encampment, and there was no time to talk further.

The camp was beneath an immense ledge of blue rock veined with white quartz and glistening with tiny bright crystals. Faolan had taken up his proper position behind the Whistler and had shifted the bone of shame from under his chin to his mouth. It would not do for any of the pack to know that the two gnaw wolves had passed the time chatting amiably.

"Beautiful, isn't it?" the Whistler whispered to Faolan, and nodded at the rock.

But Faolan couldn't answer with the bone in his mouth.

He wondered about the rock. It looked as if the stars had tumbled from the sky and rooted in the stone. A handsome black male came out from behind it and gave a gruff greeting to the Whistler and a harsh cuff to Faolan's ear. Faolan didn't mind, but it seemed so odd that, moments before, he had been enjoying the easy companionship of another wolf, and now he was once more an object of abuse.

"Lachlana and Tamsen are waiting, over there." The black wolf nodded toward the overhang of the blue rock. Faolan could see other wolves pressing through the shadows and felt their narrowed eyes clamp down on him. Their curiosity was unnerving. Before, he was the freakish wolf who had jumped for the sun, and he was now the shamed wolf who had cracked the *byrrgis*.

Off to one side, the Whistler watched the other wolves. He could tell they were amazed by Faolan's size and his vigor, for even when Faolan was groveling in the dirt, he did not look like a gnaw wolf. His coat was too sleek; there was nothing raggedy about him. They were utterly baffled.

"I've never seen such a gnaw wolf," one young male said with a tinge of envy in his voice.

The Whistler wondered what the other wolves might think if they knew that, just hours before, Faolan had ridden a buck to death. The Whistler worried about this strange young gnaw wolf. *He's outside anything they've ever imagined!*

And although Faolan immediately sank to his belly and began the crawl of humiliation toward the two out-flankers, a shadow of dignity clung to him.

Faolan caught only a glimpse of the two outflank-ers before he began crawling, but he saw that they were powerful wolves with almost identical creamy-hued pelts. He judged them to be sisters. When he reached their paws, he stopped and dropped the bone of shame. The slightly smaller wolf picked up the bone quickly, but not before giving Faolan a sharp bite to the nose. Then her sister presented him with a fresh bone, a frag-ment of an antler. This was the contrition bone he was to carve. But first the pack leader came forward to read the bone of shame. The two outflankers took several steps back.

Standing directly over Faolan's head, Dain began to read in a deep, sonorous voice, "As recorded by the gnaw wolf, Heep, of the River Pack of the MacDuncan clan..."

Faolan could not help but flinch as he heard Heep's

name spoken. *I'd better get used to this*, he thought. *I'm going to have to hear it again and again!*

"On the morning after the fifteenth night of the Caribou Moon, a *byrrgis* was assembled on the Burn in pursuit of a bull moose...."

By the fifth "humble" in Heep's story, Faolan thought he detected a snicker among the assembled wolves. This momentarily heartened Faolan, but not for long.

"He was really bad, wasn't he, Mum?" he heard a little pup say.

"Indeed!" his mum replied.

Faolan pressed his tail more tightly between his legs and shut his eyes. Why had he been such a fool? Duncan MacDuncan's words once again echoed in his ear. *You have no sense.*

I'm big but I'm stupid, Faolan thought. *Why did I ever try to do that—stand up like a grizzly?* It struck him that even Thunderheart might have been appalled by his behavior; she might have thought he had misused what she taught him. The very idea was intolerable. *How many wolves could offend not one but two species of animals?* he thought. He had never felt so disgraced in his life.

When Dain had finished reading, a silence followed that would have seemed awkward had it not been interrupted by a very young pup who burst out, "Mum, why did the wolf carve the word 'humble' so many times?" This earned the poor pup a solid thwack, and he took off squealing.

"Here, here!" Dain snarled. "We are assembled to witness the rituals of contrition, to right the wrongs given to outflankers." He turned his glare on Faolan. "Continue, gnaw wolf."

Faolan arched his back as high as possible, tucked his tail between his legs, then advanced toward the two outflankers. When this was completed, he sank to his knees and flattened his belly to the ground, then twisted his neck. Finally, he rolled on his back and presented his belly to the two outflankers. While in this position, he began to confess his error.

"I, Faolan, gnaw wolf of the Pack of the Eastern Scree, am guilty of the actions gnawed on the bone of shame by Heep. I swear by my marrow that the truth has been carved, and I am prepared to make amends by carving this bone presented to me by the estimable Lachlana and Tamsen, distinguished outflankers of the Pack of the Blue Rock."

Adair had explained to Faolan that he must carve his contrition bone with the Great Chain, and, at the precise point where his conduct had offended the order, make his mark — that of the spiraling lines of his footpad.

Faolan had been carving the Great Chain from the very first day he had joined the wolves of the Beyond. At first, gnaw wolves were expected to render a simple version of the Great Chain, but as they advanced, they learned that the chain was much more intricate, with myriads of links between classes. Because of his proficiency in gnawing, Faolan had been told to do more complicated versions of the Great Chain. He wondered if these wolves knew he was already up to the fourth order. If not, he could do the simplified version that would make for easier and quicker work.

But just at that moment, he heard the first note of a howl, a perfect note that swooped up into the night. He turned his head and was amazed to see that the sound had issued from the twisted throat of the Whistler. It rose in the darkness like a beautiful night-blooming flower. The others joined in, for they had spotted the mist of Duncan MacDuncan, and this could be the last night they would be able to see it before the Moon of the First Snow arrived and the constellation of the Great Wolf slipped away until spring.

Faolan turned his head from the bone. The old chieftain had reached the top of the star ladder. His twisted beard was neatly braided once more and he seemed to be peering right down at Faolan. *I must carve the whole chain as I know it,* he thought.

There would be no shortcuts. He studied the antler, licked it several times to become familiar with its surface, and then began to inscribe the Great Chain.

"Look at the sun he carves," someone whispered. "You almost feel the heat!"

"It's frightening — too real," said another.

Faolan tried to close his ears, but he could not help but hear a third wolf say in a quavering voice, "Could he be from the Dim World?"

Faolan had meant only to carve the bone as best he could. But it seemed that no matter how hard he tried, he never got things right. But he wouldn't stop trying; he couldn't. He would leave for the Pack of the Fire Grass at dawn.

CHAPTER NINE

THE MIST OF MACDUNCAN

BY NOW, FAOLAN KNEW THE RIT-
uals of contrition flawlessly. It didn't bother him anymore
to hear the story that Heep had carved recited aloud.
In a short course of time, he had left behind three bones
of contrition, carved so exquisitely that many wolves
began to fear he was an agent from the Dim World. But it
ceased to bother Faolan. Let them think what they would,
for no matter what they said or how they looked at his
bones, he was determined to carve as well as he could.
The wolves of the Watch were said to be the finest carv-
ers in the Beyond. And it was them he wanted to impress.
If they were true artists, they would not view his work
with superstition.

Faolan could not get out of his mind the beautiful
note the Whistler had sung when Duncan MacDuncan's

lochin reached the top of the star ladder. But why, Faolan wondered, did he seem to feel that the mist of MacDuncan still lingered even though it could no longer be seen? It was as if there was a scent trail Duncan MacDuncan was following through the stars, and it led straight to Faolan. It made no sense, but Faolan felt the mist of MacDuncan hovering just above him.

All of these thoughts were streaming through Faolan's mind when he mounted a ridge and caught sight of a wolf. Lael! The Obea of the MacDuncan clan. Faolan's breath caught in his throat. There was only one reason why she would come so far from Carreg Gaer. A *malcadh* must have been born into the River Pack, Heep's pack.

Faolan was upwind of the Obea, so she could not catch his scent. He crouched low in a ditch, peeking above the fringe of winter grass. The only scent he could detect was that of the newborn pup the Obea carried by the scruff of its neck. It must have been the pup of the mother he had seen just before the *gaddergludder*.

The Obea's sterility seemed to have affected even her urine and other scent marks. Faolan imagined that the Obeas must be bereft not only of scent and offspring but of feelings as well. Lael might as well have been carrying a clod of dirt. And even from where he crouched, he could see that her eyes were strange. They were green like the eyes of all the wolves of the Beyond, but absent of any light whatsoever—as cold and as distant as the stars. He thought of the winter stars that the wolves called the muted constellations, which appeared in the blizzard-wrapped nights of the hunger moons.

From his vantage point, he could not see any obvious deformity in the pup. He assumed that this pup's only fault was to have been born too early, for this moon was not the birthing time for wolves. Early pups, although not precisely *malcadhs*, were abandoned because they were deemed too hard to care for. More often than not, they had unseen flaws within and would soon die.

Lael climbed a very steep incline to the highest part of the ridge. She kept her pace steady. The tiny creature dangled from her muzzle, and Faolan could see its hind feet kicking weakly. When Lael reached the top, she put the pup down. Smack in the middle of an owl flight path! Faolan knew it was a route to the volcanoes, where Gwynneth gathered coals. But it was also a moose trail.

"How thoughtful!" Faolan muttered. If the owls didn't get the pup, the moose surely would. It made him shudder to think of that pup squashed under giant hooves. He hoped it would be over shortly. But he could not help wondering how long the little pup would be left mewling into the vast nothingness, how lonely it must feel.

Faolan's own recollections of abandonment were vague. He knew only what Thunderheart had told him, what she had surmised. That he had been left on the big river's edge during the time of the Moon of the Cracking Ice, and the fragment of ice on which he had been placed tore loose. He would have died had he not snagged on Thunderheart's foot. He had gone from cold and nothingness to warmth and milk and that huge booming heart. His fear of the nothingness was only faintly remembered, but he would wish it on no living creature. And yet he knew the death of a pup was a small price to pay for the health of the clan. It must be done. It was the most sacred of all the laws in the *gaddernock*.

He continued to watch the scene from the ridge. The Obea had set the pup down not just on top of the neighboring ridge but on a flat piece of table rock that looked as if it had been placed there for exactly this purpose. The perfect *tummfraw*! Then, without giving a backward glance, the Obea turned and headed down the path she had come.

Faolan was filled with an agonizing mixture of anxiety and curiosity. Did the little pup wonder what had happened to the milk scent of its mum? What was it feeling right now? Was it cold? A chill wind had blown up. Could he rescue this pup, as Thunderheart had done for him? But that was impossible for he had no milk, and it was most certainly against the codes of the wolves of the Beyond for another wolf to interfere with a *malcadh*.

When the Obea had dissolved into the gathering mist of twilight, Faolan could stand it no longer and began to move out of the ditch and make his way to the *tummfraw*. When he was almost to the top, he could hear sporadic soft whimpers from the pup. The last part of his climb seemed endless. Every step he took felt like a betrayal of the most sacred codes of wolves. But he only wanted to look.

No, this is a lie. A voice seemed to fill his head. *You want to give comfort.* By his marrow, it felt as if the mist of MacDuncan had followed him right to the top of this ridge. He looked across the starry indigo dome of the night sky. There was not a sign of the Great Wolf constellation, nor the star ladder, nor the Cave of Souls. *Then why do I feel him?*

Faolan took one more step. There was the pup, tinier than he could have imagined. She was a tawny drop of gold and perfectly formed. He had never seen anything so perfect. But so tiny that every time her heart beat, it shook her entire body. How tempted he was to lick her, to give her a momentary bit of warmth before she died. He could tell she would not live long. The first snowflakes of the season began to fall. Perhaps she would be buried under them and fall into a frozen sleep. They said it was a good way to pass from life. Yes, he wished for a blanket of heavy snow. Perhaps it would camouflage her from the owls or the prowling land animals such as bobcats and cougars. And it was doubtful that moose would take this path if the snow was deep.

He would not touch her, but from the top of the ridge, Faolan began to howl a prayer to Great Lupus, a prayer for snow.

The night has come on, the stars walk the skies,
now let the snow fall where a dying pup lies
on this tummfraw, *left with no mother, no milk,*
so cold in the night, so all alone,
with only the nothingness to call its home,
with only an emptiness as wide as the sea,

with no place to go and nothing to be.
Oh, where have you gone, Great Wolf of the night?
Oh, where have you gone, as this pup fights for her life?
Oh, what do you see from your den in the sky?
Oh, what do you see where this sweet pup does lie?
Like a tiny gold star her light grows dim,
her breath grows shallow,
her whimpers grow thin.
Spare her the tearing teeth of the fox,
spare her the ripping talons of the owl.
If take her you must, then do it so sweetly
for she cries now so softly
and her heart beats so weakly.
Let a snowy pelt cover her so thick, so white.
Then let her soul take its very last flight,
where she'll frolic and play with pups in the stars,
where bellies are full and malcadhs are fair,
where there is no hunting and hunger is gone,
where you stand on a star and can touch the sun,
where the wolves and the bears and the caribou are one.

CHAPTER TEN

THE SARK
OF THE SLOUGH

THE SARK OF THE SLOUGH WAS outside her cave building up the fire in her kiln when the bedraggled she-wolf staggered up the trail. "Oh, my!" the Sark sighed. "I'll be with you in a moment, dear."

She tossed her head toward the cave. The Sark's skittish eye, which some said was the color of a spoiled egg yolk, slid in the opposite direction. She saw a shudder pass through the she-wolf. *Well,* thought the Sark, *at least she has enough strength to be a wee bit frightened of my stupid eyeball.*

The she-wolf walked stiffly toward the mouth of the cave. She was desperate for comfort but half afraid to enter the den of this strange wolf living outside the clan, who toyed with fire and who some said was a witch. But it was the fire the Sark used to brew her potions. The forgetting potions. And the she-wolf needed to forget.

The she-wolf let her eyes adjust to the darkness, found the pile of pelts in the back, and, circling tightly three times, sank down to rest. She sniffed the fur and picked up traces of the scent of the last *malcadh* mother who had slept on the pelt. It was old, more than a year. The she-wolf was utterly exhausted, but she couldn't sleep.

Her eyes darted about the cave. It was the oddest wolf den she had ever been in. Skin bags hung on protruding spikes made from antlers, and on some ledges, there were clay pots and jugs. She had heard that the Sark knew the magic of turning earth into objects—things that could be used. The Sark was like the owls in that way, but the owls mostly used their fires for metals, not earth and clay. On the cave walls were also skins with marks that looked as if they had been scratched in with a shard of burnt wood, but the she-wolf had no idea what the marks meant. Some of them were rather pretty, however, and made pleasing designs. There were also bundles of feathers—no owl feathers but ptarmigan and other grouse arranged in bursting sheaves. The Sark even had clumps of dried grasses, herbs, and mosses hanging upside down.

The Sark came into the cave and with her teeth took a stopper from a jug lying on its side, to let a thin trickle of water spill into a small clay container beneath it. Then she shook some leaves from one of the hanging clumps. From another container she got lichen and sprinkled it over the top of the water.

"Drink that," the Sark said, pushing the mixture toward the she-wolf. "It will start the forgetting."

As soon as a *malcadh*'s mother was driven from the pack, the forgetting began. In the wake of forgetting, for a time there was a darkness deep within her where the pup had grown. And then eventually, that darkness faded to gray, so it became just a shadow of her loss, allowing her to go on, find a new clan, a new pack, and a new mate. But for some, the forgetting took longer. They teetered on the brink of the deep darkness without ever really allowing it to fill them.

The she-wolf looked gingerly at the clay bowl. It was all so odd—the bowl, the water from a jug, the bits of grasses and herbs floating in it.

"Go on, dearie, take a good swallow. Now, you're not one of those she-wolves"—the Sark avoided using the word "mum" or "mother"—"You're not one who went *by-lang*, are you?" Some pregnant she-wolves seemed to sense they were carrying a *malcadh* and went deeply away to try and escape the Obea.

"No, there wasn't time," she sobbed. "She was perfect."

"But it" — the Sark used the word "it" when referring to the pup — "it was early. No chance, my dear, and lots of problems. Now drink up."

She was careful not to say the darkness will come, for sometimes it only made the mothers resist. The Sark knew about resisting. She knew about not forgetting. But it was too late for the Sark, too late. Indeed, her whole life was dedicated to remembering. And so now, as the she-wolf became drowsy and fell into her long sleep, there was a whiff of something that stirred a dim memory for the Sark.

Aaah, yes, she thought. The she-wolf had eaten sweet grass from the high plains during the last of the summer moons. It had been during a late summer moon when the Sark had made her decision never to join a clan. It was the first time she had spotted what she felt sure had been her Milk Giver, her mother. She had been a yearling then. She resisted going to her memory jug. She was not in the mood for stirring up anguish.

The Sark's memory jugs offered their own kind of law, which was as important to her as the elaborate, complicated codes and traditions of the Great Chain or the *gaddernock* were to the clan wolves. She did not need some high-ranking wolf to tell her how to bow to rank. She felt that the veneration and submission rituals were excessive to the point of being ridiculous.

Memory was sacred to the Sark, not empty rituals, and although she understood the need for the laws of the Beyond, they often seemed as dead to her as the bones they were carved on. Memory was alive in the way a river is alive and flowing. But this river was flowing not with water but with the tributaries of scent. It was the scent that brought the memories.

The Sark believed that if there was no memory, the bones that contained the *gaddernock* would crumble to dust. Most of the rituals of the wolves made no sense to her. What the Sark sought were experiences, feelings, and colors. Too often, life for the wolves of the Beyond was only about hunting and the elaborate social codes of the clans. Without memory, there could only be indifference. Without memory, there could only be blind obedience. Without memory, there could be no true con-sciousness, and the wolves of the Beyond would live in a walled, colorless world without meaning. She peered into the deep shadows of the cave, where her memory jugs stood like sentries of her past. Then she glanced at the mother of the *malcadh*. The she-wolf was sleeping deeply and would for two days. She would awake ravenous and go out to hunt. She would leave, and she would not look back.

CHAPTER ELEVEN

"SHE'LL KNOW ME!"

THE SNOW FAOLAN HAD PRAYED
for had not come. A foul, gusting wind had brought sleet
and rain and then more sleet. But sleet was no camouflage. If only there had been a heavy snowfall! Faolan
tried not to think of the tearing teeth and claws that
might find their way to the pup. He saw a small herd of
caribou with their rumps pointed into the weather and
was not even tempted to chase one. He could not feel
hunger. He could feel only deep sorrow for the creature
he had left dying on the ridge.

He made his way down a winding trail into the shallow basin that led to the Slough and the odd wolf who
lived there. He was very curious about her. She lived
alone and though wolves came to her for embers and tonics, they were deeply superstitious about her powers. *Did*

they see moon rot in her eyes? he wondered. He had a sense that, though she lived apart from the wolves, she was wise in their ways. He might learn something from her, something that would help him in the *gaddergnaw*. And he could talk to her about the *malcadh*. He had a compelling need to speak about the little tawny pup.

At the entrance to the Slough, Faolan caught his first scent of smoke and then saw a thread winding up from what appeared to be a domed earthen lodge. He had found the Sark of the Slough's camp. The cave in which she lived was surrounded by a cleared area where she kept her various fires. It was different from Gwynneth the Rogue smith owl's open-forge fire. The Sark had built little dens to shelter her fires.

The Sark seemed to be waiting for him. Faolan had been downwind of the Sark, so he was uncertain how she had caught his scent, unless she had caught it hours before when he had still been coming down the ridge, and the wind had been blowing in a different direction. His first reaction was one of shame, for he was walking up that path with Heep's bone of contrition still gripped in his teeth. As the Sark stepped forward, Faolan set down the bone and immediately sank to his knees, then to his belly. He was profoundly embarrassed. The last time they had seen each other was at the wall of fire, where the Sark had defended his triumphant leap and fumed at the chieftains, calling them idiots for chasing him down without evidence that he had the foaming-mouth disease. And now what was he? Nothing more than a disgraced gnaw wolf sent on a trail of shame.

"Surely" — the Sark began to speak in her raggedy voice, which seemed always to have a snarl embedded in its center — "you are not pulling that old V-and-O stuff with me."

"V and O?"

"Veneration and Obeisance. The submission rituals."

"Actually, these are the contrition rituals. I violated the *byrrgnock*, the laws governing the *byrrgis*."

"I know, I know. You don't have to explain to me what the *byrrgnock* is or what you've done. I could have predicted it," she said scornfully, although Faolan wasn't sure if the scorn was directed at him. "Get up, for Lupus' sake. I have little tolerance for these displays." She nodded toward the mouth of the cave, where another fire burned at the entrance. "Go inside. I have to get these pots out of the kiln."

The fire in the cave threw off a great heat. Faolan was just about to settle in as close as possible, when he noticed a sleeping she-wolf on the pile of hides and caught her scent. The mother of the *malcadh*! Faolan began to tremble. He stood stiff-legged, his ears laid flat, his eyes narrowed. He could not shift his gaze from the she-wolf.

"Don't worry; she's asleep," the Sark said, entering the cave.

"I saw her pup on the ridge."

"I know."

"How?"

"I smelled her on you."

"But I didn't touch her. I swear!"

"I know that, too." The Sark moved around him, carrying something in a skin bag. Perhaps it was the pot she had mentioned. But he wasn't interested. He couldn't take his eyes off the mother of the *malcadh*.

"Did my mother come here when...when..." Faolan felt as if he were tipping at the edge of the universe, about to fall into an abyss. But if his mother were still alive, he would have everything! He would find her. He would run beyond the Beyond to the farthest ends of the earth.

"When the Obea took you?"

Faolan nodded.

"No." The Sark was glad she didn't have to lie. She would have lied if Faolan's mother had come, but thankfully she hadn't. The Sark was contemptuous of many of the wolf conventions, but she believed that the less a *malcadh* knew about his birth mother, the better. Still, the Sark knew she was in for a rough time with this young wolf.

"Why do they do it?"

"You know why, Faolan. Don't be stupid! It's one of the few things the clans do that does make sense. It is for the health of the bloodlines."

Faolan wheeled around and glared. "I'm tired of hearing that!" he growled. "None of this makes sense to me, and it isn't just the laws for *malcadhs*. I...I..." he stammered, but then it all poured out. "I'm more alone now than when I was out on my own." The Sark seemed to be only half listening, busy with something at the edge of the cave that he couldn't see. He looked at her. She was different and alone and yet she seemed so content. He wanted desperately for the Sark to pay attention to him, to understand his pain, to—

She could never wrap herself around him like the huge and gentle Thunderheart, and he was embarrassed that the thought had ever crossed his mind. He was too big for all that. But once he had been a small, furry pup, and comfort came so easily to him. Once he had been dear to someone, cherished. He looked again at the Sark. Had she ever been dear to anyone, cuddled, loved?

He couldn't stand being so close to creatures like himself yet feeling so apart. He was connected to a clan and yet not a member, connected to a pack yet scorned. He recalled that he had thought—before MacDuncan told him of the *gaddergnaw*—that it might have been better to leave, to go to Ga'Hoole. To start somehow all over again. He sighed loudly. "I am just so tired of them and their stupid ways."

"Well, go ahead, be tired!" the Sark replied. She was busy arranging her pots in a niche. Faolan cocked his head with sudden interest. The pots were curious objects, odd and beautiful. There were small, colorful stones embedded in some of their surfaces, and decorative markings. But he did not want to be distracted.

"Did you know my mother? My father?"

The Sark turned toward him, her skittering eye spinning madly. Her fur was always in some sort of disarray, but now her hackles rose up in a little private storm of their own, adding to the wildness of her pelt. She spoke slowly, as if she were addressing a pup who was not very bright. "Don't you understand? I am packless. I am clanless. I have no friends, no associates. I don't know any wolves."

"But they seek you out. The clans did when they came after me."

"Yes, and that was a big mistake. I should have demanded more evidence that you had the foaming-mouth disease."

Faolan nodded toward the she-wolf. "She came to you."

"It's different. They come in need. Not to chew the bone, not to howl. Your mother did not come here. I did not know her."

Faolan whimpered and settled down with his muzzle buried between his paws.

"Stop whimpering. I can't stand whimperers."

Faolan snuffed. "I just want to know, that's all. I had a Milk Giver, you know. A second one after the Obea took me."

"I know, a grizzly."

"How did you know?"

"I picked up her scent when the *byrrgis* was tracking you. So did the others. Except they thought it was a foaming-mouth grizzly that had bitten you and given you the disease."

"But you didn't?"

"I wasn't sure, really. As I said, not enough evidence. But I did pick up the scent of milk—long-ago milk."

Faolan thought this strange wolf must have the most extraordinary sense of smell imaginable. "But if you picked up the scent of my second Milk Giver, why would you think she would ever bite me? I was like Thunderheart's own pup. Even if she were crazy with the foaming-mouth disease, she would never have bitten me."

The Sark cocked her head, and for a moment the skittering eye grew still. She looked not at Faolan but at the ground. "Oh," she whispered wearily, "you would not believe what a Milk Giver can do."

"What do you mean?"

The Sark considered for what seemed a long time and slowly turned her head toward the very back of the cave, where the darkest shadows collected and where some of her first memory jars perched in niches.

She did not realize that Faolan had been watching her carefully.

"What are those things?"

She angled her head so that her skittering eye was pointed toward the jug and turned her steady eye on Faolan. "Those are my memory jugs."

"Your memory jugs? Do you have any memories of *gaddergnaws*?"

"No. Why do you want to know?"

"There's to be one when the Singing Grass Moon comes."

"If it ever comes." She shook her head wearily.

"What do you mean?"

"Something is *cag mag* with the weather these days. The seasons. I've been trying to figure it out." She sighed. "So they're having another *gaddergnaw*? It's been a while."

"Yes, and this could be my chance." He hesitated to say that Duncan MacDuncan had told him this.

"Your chance for what?"

"To get out. To become a wolf of the Watch. I thought you might have some memories and some advice that could help me."

"You'll need a better reason than just getting out, dearie!"

"What do you mean?"

"I mean exactly what I said. Getting out is a stupid reason. Where are you going? I don't need to stick my snout into any pot for that advice." She raised a paw and tapped her head. "It's right here in the old noggin. You've been in my den long enough. You must leave before she wakes. It will be too painful for her if she smells her pup on you."

"All right," Faolan replied. He rose up, thinking again of his first Milk Giver. He had no hope of finding Thunderheart on this earth. He would not find her until he died and made his way to that place the bears called Ursulana and the wolves called the Cave of Souls. But his own wolf mother or wolf father could still be alive.

The Sark must have read his mind.

She gave a low growl. "Don't do it, Faolan. Don't go looking for your mother. She won't recognize you, for one thing. And then how will you feel?"

"Oh, she'll know me. She'll recognize me," he said with a steely certainty. "In her marrow, she'll know it's me when she sees this." And he picked up his front foot and ground it into the dirt, once again leaving the imprint of his splayed paw with its spiral pattern.

CHAPTER TWELVE

AN ABOMINATION!

THE WIND WAS NOT COOPERATING.
It seemed to be out of sorts, as could often happen during
the Moon of the First Snow. Gwynneth, Rogue smith and
daughter of the late Gwyndor, had spent the better part
of the night tacking against it to go north toward the
Ring of Sacred Volcanoes. As was also customary during
this season, the volcanoes had become active. Gwynneth
could now gather "bonk" coals, the old smithy term for
the coals that burned the hottest, the ones with blue cen-
ters ringed with green.

Gwynneth had planned to get to the volcanoes early
in this snow moon, ahead of the other owls from the
Hoolian kingdoms to the south. She had taken a round-
about route to avoid stalling out in the cantankerous
headwinds.

An updraft of slightly warmer air came out of nowhere and allowed her a brief respite in her battle against the shifting winds. She was able to soar effortlessly while being pulled vaguely in her intended direction. It was a welcome break for her wings, but as she soared, her ears caught a thin filament of sound weaving through the winds. The sound was curious yet slightly alarming—tiny mewling whimpers. She began to cock her head this way and then that. Masked Owls were members of the Barn Owl family, known for their exceptional hearing. Because of the uneven placement of their ear slits, they were able to scoop up the smallest traces of sound. Furthermore, these owls could expand and contract their facial discs, which allowed them to focus in precisely on the source of the sound.

The mewling had now become an agonizing shriek accompanied by a horrifying ripping. *Great Glaux! A pup is being murdered! By . . . by . . . by a wolf!* Gwynneth knew that of all the complicated codes and laws of these wolves, murdering a *malcadh* was the worst offense of all. It was an abomination!

And Gwynneth knew the killer was a wolf. She recognized the sound of the gnashing teeth. The long front fangs were for ripping, and soon she heard the slicing sounds of the back teeth, working like blades to cut the flesh into tinier pieces. She could see nothing, for the cloud cover was thick, but she knew what was happening from the horrible noises and the panting of the murdering wolf.

Gwynneth fell into what owls called a kill plunge. Although it was now a life plunge, a rescue plunge, if she could save the little pup and beat off the murderer. *If . . . if . . . if . . .*

But it was too late. Just as Gwynneth broke out of the clouds, the wolf raced off the ridge. By the time Gwynneth lighted down on the table rock, the pup was dead. Gwynneth looked in horror at its body. It was a tiny little thing, a female and not really a *malcadh*. "Just born too soon," Gwynneth whispered softly. The pup's body had been ripped apart. *Why didn't the wolf smother her?* Gwynneth wondered. This death was unspeakably violent. The wolf had bitten all the way though to the pup's tiny bones.

Gwynneth was seized by a sudden revulsion and had to yarp a pellet. Many owls came across *malcadhs* left on the *tummfraws* of their flight paths and ate them. Gwynneth had given up this practice when she had come to live in the Beyond. Never, however, would an owl tear apart a pup so mercilessly, so brutally. Usually, a quick stab of the beak at the soft place in the pup's skull finished them off quickly. This *malcadh*, however, had not died quickly but in unimaginable agony.

Oh, she thought, *might it swiftly find its way to the Cave of Souls.* Gwynneth knew that the Great Wolf constellation was not visible, nor would it be for another two moons. But, surely, the Star Wolf would be moved not to let this poor little pup's soul wander aimlessly.

Gwynneth's first instinct, though irrational, was to take the pup's bones and fly them herself to the Cave of Souls. But of course the Great Wolf constellation was gone, and who ever heard of any animal getting such a shortcut to their heaven? In the rational part of her mind, she knew that the *malcadh*'s suffering on earth was over and would not follow her in death. With the last breath the little pup took, her suffering ended and her soul was severed painlessly from her body, as painlessly as the shedding of the undercoat during the summer moons. But when Gwynneth looked upon the torn body of this pup, she experienced profound pain and revulsion. She felt her gut wrench and had the urge to yarp another pellet, but there was nothing left inside her. She felt as hollow as her bones.

Gwynneth told herself she must be practical. There was nothing she could do here. She still had a long way to fly to the Sacred Volcanoes, and she had to get there during the first flares. Otherwise, where would she be? A Rogue smith without two bonk embers to rub together!

Gwynneth began to spread her wings to lift off but then folded them again. In the high, piercing cries of the Masked Owl, she began to sing the owl song for when a nestling died.

> *May Glaux bless you and keep you always,*
> *may you leave your pain behind,*
> *may you fledge your wings so quickly*
> *and climb to the night sublime,*
> *may you look down and see we love you*
> *and though you never will grow old,*
> *but forever stay so young,*
> *may you know that it's for you*
> *that this song is sung.*

CHAPTER THIRTEEN

THE DARK
VALE DESCENDS

BY THE TIME FAOLAN HAD COMPLETED the trail of shame and returned to his pack on the Eastern Scree, the Moon of the Frost Stars had already risen in the skies.

Snow had fallen at last. The slopes of the Eastern Scree that ran down from Crooked Back Ridge billowed like snow clouds. The ridge was sheathed in ice and cut through the billows like a crystal knife slicing the flawless blue sky. Many claimed that the Moon of the Frost Stars was the coldest of all the hunger moons of winter, and because of this, tempers were short. Quarrels broke out frequently within the pack, and gnaw wolves provided a convenient vessel for other wolves' frustrations. Faolan was sore from the bites and thrashings he had received. If the wolves were successful in tracking down prey, the animals were so winter-thin that there was no meat to spare for a gnaw wolf. On this frigid day, they had managed to bring down a red deer. After they had eaten their fill, the pack wolves tossed the rumen, the deer's first stomach with its cud of undigested grasses and lichens, to the gnaw wolves.

The wolves scorned the rumen and loathed the taste of the fibrous vegetation, but Faolan had become accustomed to eating such foods. When he was a tiny pup, he went foraging with Thunderheart in the early spring for onion bulbs and anything else that sprouted from the earth and had slipped the lock of winter. Thunderheart would first chew up the bulbs or grasses very thoroughly, often swallowing them if they were especially tough and then regurgitating them for Faolan's consumption, as wolf parents do with meat for their cubs. Faolan figured he could do this himself. He chewed until the partially digested vegetation of the rumen was a fine mash, then swallowed it. It tasted no different to him from when Thunderheart had done the same.

For wolves, eating vegetation was unimaginable. It was not meat. When tossed the rumen, a gnaw wolf would eat only the intestinal tissue and leave the vegetation behind. But Faolan ate it all. And because he did, his coat remained glossy, and he appeared no thinner than before. This only added to Faolan's strangeness in the eyes of the other wolves.

Ever since Faolan had returned from the Sark's cave, he had been obsessed with dreams of his first Milk Giver. He wondered if he had siblings, and if so, were they normal and had they survived? Where might they be now? They would have been allowed to stay in the pack and have been fostered by another she-wolf with milk to spare, for that was the rule. Would they resemble him except for his splayed paw?

All of these questions haunted Faolan as he went about the business of becoming a dutiful gnaw wolf. He accepted the abuse with the appropriate whimpering and slid through the submission postures as if he had them engraved in his own marrow and not simply on the bones he was tediously ordered to gnaw. The one question to which he most often returned was where his parents might have gone. The harder Faolan tried to think about these questions, the more elusive the answers became. He felt as if he were tumbling through a deep vale of shadows.

On an evening during the last crescent of the second hunger moon, a she-wolf far in MacDonegal territory was haunted by a scent she had discovered in the skull of a grizzly bear almost a year before. As soon as she had sniffed that scent, the forgetting had stopped. Like the ice slides of spring that peeled back the ground leaving raw, exposed earth, she felt suddenly vulnerable to memories, to feelings that had been long frozen, locked beneath the cold, snowy mantle of winter. The barriers that had built up so carefully deep within her and served as invisible scar tissue were swept away. Memories crashed in with a crushing force. *He was silver, my only silver one.*

In all the litters Morag had borne, she had never had a pup with a silver pelt. There had been three pups in this litter, two tawny females and then the silver one with the splayed paw. She had, for those brief hours before the Obea found them, mothered him, nursed him, and adored nuzzling her nose deep into his pelt. It was a pelt of singular beauty, for it looked as if stars had fallen from the sky and been swirled through the fur. She would have named him for a constellation, perhaps Skaarsgard, the leaping wolf who caught wolf pups who fell off the star ladder on their way to the Cave of Souls.

It was said that for mothers of *malcadhs*, a darkness

invaded their bodies where the pup had grown in their womb and that gradually this darkness faded until it became a pale gray shadow. But the pale gray shadow was changing, blackening; a darkness was invading not just her womb but her head as well.

During the time of forgetting, Morag had gone on and done what mothers of *malcadhs* were supposed to do. She had found a new clan, the MacDonegals, a new mate, and borne another litter, of three healthy red-furred pups. She had become an outflanker of some repute in the clan, and though her legs were still strong and she could run at attack speed for long distances, the darkness now seemed to be invading her vision.

On her last *byrrgis*, the point wolf had given the signal for attack speed. Morag flashed out to the front of the outflankers, her usual position. The musk ox herd appeared like a storm cloud lifting from the horizon. It was her job with the other outflanker to begin to turn the herd east toward the rising sun, which would be blinding. But it seemed as if the blinding was already happening. The storm cloud that was the herd remained a blur even as they drew closer. Morag felt as if she were sinking into a haze. How would she ever spot the weak musk ox that must be split off from the herd? That had always been her strength. Morag could run at top speed while still scanning the herd to find the sick one, the old one, the dying animal. Musk ox were slow compared to caribou or red deer. She should be able to spot the *cailleach*. She suddenly felt herself trip. She was down. She felt the packers streak by her. *Great Lupus. I have fallen!* She knew that her life as an outflanker had just ended.

CHAPTER FOURTEEN

THE RED DEER OF
THE YELLOW SPRINGS

MHAIRIE WAS STREAKING OUT ON
the west flank of a large herd of red deer. This was her
chance to earn her position and—Lupus be praised—the
gnaw wolf seemed to have learned his lesson. He was
safely behind her, far behind her, but she would not look
now. Once again, she had been sent to run with the Pack
of the Eastern Scree, the River Pack, and the Blue Rock
Pack when a herd had been spotted near Blue Rock territory in the last of the hunger moons. This time, Alastrine
and Stellan had been sent from the Carreg Gaer to
accompany Mhairie. She was being observed carefully.
She had to perform flawlessly, and if that cursed gnaw
wolf acted up, she would personally sink her teeth into
the most tender part of his muzzle and enjoy every second of it.

They were chasing the herd through a region known as the Yellow Springs. A signal had been passed for the crimping maneuver to commence. They were going to turn the herd slightly and then split it. This was a risky maneuver, but with a herd this large, they had little choice. There was no way to spot the weak ones, who stayed in the middle of the herd as long as possible. Faolan could see Stellan close to Mhairie, passing signals to her. Within seconds, Mhairie had spotted a *cailleach*. Now Faolan's job was to close in and pick up any urine or scat scents that did not seem healthy.

What a miserable task I have, he thought as he saw Mhairie pressing forward toward the *cailleach*, then suddenly slowing her pace to a casual lope as if she had lost interest. The red deer would slow down a bit, but soon Mhairie would be back with Stellan and another outflanker.

It was a strategy Faolan had used when he brought down a caribou alone a year before. Except there had been no captain passing signals, no outflankers to help press the crimp. He had done it all by himself.

It was the endgame now. They had the old *cailleach* surrounded. She stood looking bewildered as blood spurted from wounds on her haunches. These wounds were enough to bring her to a stop, but not to kill her. For that, they had to get to her neck and the vital life-pumping artery. Mhairie and the other outflankers hung back. Their job was done. Some of the largest males encircled the *cailleach* and began to charge her in relays, but she reared up and struck one with her hooves.

"The nerve!" muttered Heep.

"Yes, magnificent!" It was a windy gust from the Whistler's crooked throat.

The Whistler had spoken the thought that was in Faolan's own head. How had this old female found the strength of spirit to rise up and strike out at these four immense wolves?

"It's magnificent. The *cailleach* has a wonderful spirit," the Whistler continued.

"May it flee her body soon so as not to fatigue our own magnificent superiors, the captain, and the sublieu-tenants," Heep said loudly.

The Whistler gave Heep a withering look. "Oh, just go stick your face in some musk ox scat!"

Faolan was about to laugh but was shocked when Heep sank to his knees in front of the Whistler.

"Oh, dear Whistler, I humbly beg your pardon." His pointy nostrils were expanding and contracting nervously while he ground the side of his face into the dirt. "I would never propose to elevate myself above this great and dignified beast who is dying to provide life for our exalted superiors. If I have given offense, I most humbly beg your forgiveness. For it is only through the rich meat of this noble deer that our leaders, our great and heroic chieftains, and our glorious packs will prosper."

But the Whistler had wandered off to have a closer view of the moment when the red deer's life would end.

Faolan stood transfixed by Heep's display. Despite the extravagant apology, there was something horribly wrong in what he was doing. *He does not mean to give offense?* Faolan wondered. And yet Heep did give offense in some strange way. It seemed like a perversion of *lochinvyrr*. In *lochinvyrr*, words were never spoken aloud. Thanks should be expressed simply — silently — and with profound feeling, so as not to lessen the value of the life sacrificed.

Faolan began to walk away toward the circle of wolves that surrounded the red deer. Everyone had fallen silent now. There was no barking nor joyful yips, just a deep and respectful quiet. The captain had sunk to his knees in a posture of complete submission. He looked directly into the eyes of the dying animal, for there could be only truth at this moment. When the *lochinvyrr* was complete, he rose up and, without uttering a word, tore into the deer's belly to begin the sharing out of the meat.

Faolan stood in the shadows of the sparse birch grove and watched the division of the meat. The first to eat were the leaders of the pack, second came the captains of the *byrrgis*, including the outflankers. Mhairie was allowed to go first, for she had been important in initiating the crimp. There was much whooping and howling when she came forward to receive her share of the rich liver. As was customary for a young wolf who had proved herself for the first time, the other outflankers pounced on her and rubbed her head and face in the thick blood of the liver. When she rose up, her tawny face was a mask of red through which her bright green eyes shone.

"A red deer for a red wolf!" someone barked. There would be howling all through the night, for the *cailleach* was fatter than they had originally thought. The smell of blood, of torn muscles, ripped intestines, and stripped fresh bones filled the air. In the midst of this chaos of meat and blood, Mhairie suddenly stepped up to Faolan in the birch grove.

"Here," she said, and dropped a bone, a femur from the upper hind leg. "You did well today. You would honor me by gnawing the story of my first kill as an outflanker.

You might call it"—she looked down almost bashfully—"Mhairie at the Hunt of the Red Deer in Yellow Springs."

"Yes, I might." For the only privilege a gnaw wolf had was to name the account he or she inscribed on a bone. Heep had entitled Faolan's bone of shame "The Sins and Humiliation of the Gnaw Wolf Faolan." Then he had gone on to subtitle it "One Gnaw Wolf's Horrifying Violations of the *Byrrgnock*."

"Well," Mhairie said, looking up at Faolan through the blood mask of her fur. "I just wanted to say that, you know…you let me do what I wanted to do. I know you can run fast, really fast"—she paused—"for a male, that is. So, thanks." She turned and walked away.

"'So, thanks,' she says. I'm fast for a male—Urskadamus!" Faolan muttered. He hardly felt it merited his saying, "You're welcome, Mhairie, for your overwhelming gratitude."

CHAPTER FIFTEEN

ONE TINY BONE

THE SETTING MOON GLOWED RED, as if it had been dipped in the blood of the *cailleach*, and slipped down behind the western horizon. The stars were out, and the first paw of the Great Wolf was beginning to show again, which always was a cause for celebration among the clans of the Beyond. The second of the spring moons, the Moon of the Singing Grass, was when the *gaddergnaw* was to be held. But as Faolan set himself on course to travel to the *tummfraw*, he was not thinking about anything but finding the bones of the little tawny wolf.

He had come to a decision. He planned to make a *drumlyn* to honor the pup. When he found enough bones, he would take them and arrange them in a mound, the *drumlyn*, from which the little pup's spirit could spring to the first rung of the star ladder and run to the Cave of Souls.

Faoloan climbed to the very top of the ridge where he had seen the little pup on a table rock. He looked around for a bit, and then it struck him that if indeed the pup's bones had been left behind, they would most likely have slid down the slope. It had not snowed as he had prayed it would, but he remembered that it had rained heavily after he left the dying pup.

Faolan looked down the slope and tried to figure out where tiny bones might have traveled. The winter had been the coldest in memory, but there had not been many heavy snowfalls, and now at the end of the last of the winter moons, there had been more rain. So he decided to look for bones in the small rills made by the rain.

He searched long into the night until the sky began to lighten. Just as the horizon turned a dusky pink, he saw something very white poking from the soil. He carefully dug around it with his claws, then sheathed his teeth, using his lips to clamp on to it and pull it out of the ground. He set it down and stared at it. Was it a tiny rib? As he looked closer, he saw deep gashes that made his marrow tremble. A low growl began to rumble within him, a growl of anguish and wrath.

The hackles on his ruff stiffened. Whatever predator had taken this tiny wolf pup's life had done so in a most violent manner. The surface of the bone was obliterated behind a blizzard of slashing marks. It was almost impossible to make out which animal had been the predator. *Well*, Faolan thought, *it does not matter anymore.* He had the bone. He would safeguard it and then come back to find others.

The only place he could think to leave the bone was with Thunderheart's paw bone. It would give him ease to know that this tiny rib was resting with Thunderheart. He decided to take the bone there straightaway. Now he knew for certain that the little pup was done with her terrible agony, although it pained him to think of the violence of her end. But surely with the Star Wolf returning, the pup could climb the ladder to the Cave of Souls. And Faolan vowed that he would return to the slope beneath the ridge to find more of her bones — *her* bones. Faolan refused to think of the pup as an *it*, the way the Sark always spoke of *malcadhs*.

The following evening, he returned to the ridge. When he first arrived, he experienced a vague sensation that there might be another animal nearby. He lifted his nose to the wind but could not detect a scent. It was very possible that other wolves were around, for he was not that far from the Fire Grass Pack. There might be hunters out tracking the other half of the red deer herd.

The evening was dark and moonless. There was no light for casting shadows, and yet Faolan felt shadows all about him. He scolded himself for being so jumpy. *I'm becoming as superstitious as these clan wolves,* he thought, and set himself to his task.

He found several more bones from the little pup, all with deep gashes. Despite terrible lacerations, one in particular had a lovely shape and seemed almost to beg to have the pup's short little life recorded on it. So Faolan began to gnaw on it. He had not been carving for long before he felt for the first time ever a discomfort with incising a story on bone.

I can't do this yet, he thought. *The little pup's story is not complete.* It seemed wrong to carve it, almost as if the violence that had been wreaked on this bone tangled the poetry of his marking. He had to stop.

Faolan found several more bones, too many to be carried in one trip to Thunderheart's paw. He would go now with the first load, and by the time he came back for the second, perhaps he would feel differently and finish the carving.

But when he came back, the partially carved bone had disappeared. An uneasy feeling swept through him. Had another animal seen him here? And why would it take that bone and not any of the others he had left behind?

When Faolan returned to the clan, merriment was still swirling from the hunt two days before. The smell of the blood had receded somewhat. There were piles of bones to be gnawed by the three gnaw wolves. Faolan turned his attention to the femur that Mhairie had presented.

The Moon of the Frost Stars had slipped away now for good. The first thin wisp of the Cracking Ice Moon was rising. Alastrine joined Greer, the *skreeleen* of the River Pack, in baying to the rise of the first spring moon and celebrating the end of the hunger moons of winter. And then, at the height of the night, a torrential rain began, and the sky crackled with lightning that looked like the splinters of hundreds of tiny white bones.

The two *skreeleens* began to howl the *ceilidh fyre*, or the sky dance of fire. Tonight, they cried out the story of Skaarsgard, the leaping wolf who helps little ones up the star ladder. Was this not a sign that indeed the tiny pup was on her way? Faolan hoped it was an omen that all would be well and he could sleep peacefully, lulled by the little pup playing with her mates in the Cave of Souls.

But the *skreeleens* told the story of a stubborn little wolf pup who kept scampering down the star ladder. It was an old favorite, a call-and-response tale in which the little pup was not a *malcadh* but one who had simply died. Alastrine sang the part of Skaarsgard, and Greer the part of the little pup.

Skaarsgard calls: "Why do you go, little pup, little pup?"

Little pup responds: "I go to eat the meat of the fox my mum will catch come spring."

Skaarsgard calls: "But you need no meat in the soul cave, little pup, little pup."

Little pup responds: "But I have not tasted the salmon that swim in the river."

Skaarsgard calls: "But you have left your teeth behind, little pup, little pup. You are a spirit so free, your soul has risen, little pup, little pup. Leave your meat dreams behind, little pup, little pup."

Little pup responds: "I can have no dreams because I have not tasted meat. Let me eat. Let me eat."

Skaarsgard calls: "But you cannot be starving, for you

have no hunger. You have no teeth. You have no stomach. You are a soul on the star ladder."

Little pup responds: "But I am hungry."

Skaarsgard calls: "For what can you hunger?"

Little pup responds: "For dreams I'll never have. For meat I'll never eat. For rivers I'll never swim."

It was the first time Faolan had ever heard this tale. He did not find it as amusing as the other wolves did. And the sleep that he thought would come to him upon finding bones from the tiny *malcadh* did not. Instead, his sleep was ragged, shredded with visions of the little pup on the ridge falling back down to earth, not for the meat of a fox, not for the salmon in the river, but for vengeance.

When he awoke near dawn, his footpads were damp and encrusted with salt. Salt from night sweat. Foul-dream sweat. Fear sweat.

CHAPTER SIXTEEN

THE HAZE
OF MORAG

BRANGWEN WATCHED HIS MATE, Morag, walk out stiff-legged from the large cave they shared with their three yearlings in the westernmost part of the MacDonegal territory. They belonged to the Pack of the Dancing Giants, named for the dozen or more large stone formations that stood upright on the high plain near where they had their dens. Morag had gone out to chase after Brecco, the middle pup of her threesome, who had brought a bleeding hare into the cave. This was against all the rules. It was good that Brecco had become a proficient hunter, but his manners were deplorable. Did he want to invite a larger, fiercer animal right into their den?

Brangwen's first instinct was to chase after Brecco himself and give him a good cuff on the ears. But Morag had quickly jumped up and said, "No, I'll go." He knew he had to let her try. Ever since she had stumbled during the musk ox *byrrgis*, she had been out of sorts. She must be scared of falling, for she moved slowly, tentatively, like a very old wolf. This litter was probably her last, but many she-wolves, especially outflankers like Morag, still had a lot of chase left in them.

Brangwen winced now as he saw Morag bump into one of the immense upright stones. Brecco looked back at his mum and saw what had happened. The look of shock in the yearling's eyes was like a stab to Brangwen's marrow.

I must not rush out. I must let her do this herself. He watched Brecco approach his mother. Brecco's ears were laid back, his tail tucked so tightly between his legs that Brangwen thought he looked like that loathsome yellow gnaw wolf from the MacDuncan River Pack. Morag snarled and commenced scolding the yearling. She cuffed him, but Brangwen could tell that her marrow wasn't in it. Brecco stood there for several seconds as if demanding that she cuff him again, harder. But Morag turned away and walked back to the cave.

When she entered, she said nothing but circled twice and settled on the pelt of a caribou. Her eyes were half closed. Brangwen could only see thin slits of green, and he realized the green was not as bright as before. There seemed to be a film over it. He settled himself on another pelt close by.

The sun at this time of year flooded directly into the cave until it sank below the horizon. As the pale violet shadows of twilight seeped into the cave, Brangwen thought his mate had fallen asleep. But she had not. She had been thinking of how to handle the twilight that was slowly creeping through her and what she must tell Brangwen.

It had begun long before the stumble in the *byrrgis*. It had begun when the pups were still in the whelping den and she had set out to find a new den for them. She had ranged farther than she had intended, and before she knew it, she was out of the MacDonegal territory and crossing the big river. But it had felt so good to roam after being penned up with those rambunctious pups.

It was shortly after she had crossed the river that she found the skull of a grizzly bear, and seconds later, a scent came to her, dim but immediately recognizable as that of the beautiful silver pup with the stars in his fur.

That was when the darkness began. It didn't seem possible that memory should dim her vision. And to complicate matters, she had never told Brangwen about her life in the MacDuncan clan. She had not wanted to lie, but the forgetting had truly worked back then. She had no memory of that pup or his siblings when she met her new mate.

It had worked. The words kept running through her mind. *Worked.* She had rehearsed so many ways how to tell her mate, but now she simply began.

"Brangwen," she said quietly. He started, for he had thought her asleep. "The forgetting has stopped."

"What? What are you talking about? Forgetting what?"

She should have realized that males did not really know about this in the way females did, even if they had been the fathers of *malcadhs*. She closed her eyes tightly. It seemed that now she could sometimes see better with her eyes shut. "Brangwen, you must believe I am no double-tongued wolf. I would never lie to you."

"Of course not. How could you ever think such a thing, Morag?"

And so she told him about what had happened to her before they met, when she had given birth to the silver-coated *malcadh*.

"A *malcadh*," he whispered with disbelief. "And our pups so healthy."

"Because we make good pups, you and I together," she said softly.

"We certainly do." He came over, and began licking his mate's face. He could taste the oily tears that leaked from her eyes.

"I would have told you, but, you see, the forgetting works. It worked so well until, until—"

"Until you found the scent of your son, the silver one."

Morag looked at Brangwen through her filmy eyes. He didn't call the pup a *malcadh*. Not an *it*, but a *son*. "Oh, Brangwen, you called him my son."

"Of course. I might not be a female. I cannot claim ever to have birthed a pup, let alone one taken by an Obea to a *tummfraw*. But I can feel things." He paused. "And I know that this silver pup you never named burns like a bright little star inside you."

"How can you feel all this?" she said in a trembling voice.

"We are paw fast, are we not?"

"That we are!" Morag replied vigorously.

"We made our paw-fast vows—was it two autumns ago during the Caribou Moon?"

"No, the Red Leaf Moon. I remember." And then, in just a whisper, "I remember too much."

"We must talk now," Brangwen said with his head nuzzled close to the ear he had just been licking. "You must tell me about your eyes. What is happening?"

"The darkness that was in my womb where the silver pup grew has come back and spread to my eyes."

"And so you only see blackness. Is it like night always?"

"No, it is more like sinking into a haze. But I am sinking fast." She paused. "I have had time to think about this, Brangwen. I must go to the Sark of the Slough."

She could feel his hackles rise. Males were always more frightened of the Sark of the Slough than females. Her powers disturbed them. Morag had not gone to the Sark after her own loss. Perhaps she should have, she thought now. The Sark was said to have potions that helped with the forgetting, and tonics that healed the womb so it would be ready and eager for a new litter. But now she must go to the Sark to lift the haze.

"I shall go with you," Brangwen said firmly.

"You are not afraid of the Sark?" Morag asked.

"I am more afraid of you stumbling or becoming lost."

"But scents come to me more quickly now. More sharply than ever."

"You cannot smell a hole and you cannot smell your way to the Sark," Brangwen said.

"Yes, I suppose you are right. What about the yearlings? Who shall take care of them?"

"Their auntie Daraigh, of course," Brangwen answered.

"She's so strict."

He was about to say, *Not as strict as you used to be.* But he held his tongue.

And so it was decided. They would leave at dawn for the Slough and the camp of the Sark.

CHAPTER SEVENTEEN

THE GIZZARD OF GWYNNETH

AT THE SAME DAWN HOUR THAT Morag and her mate set out for the Sark of the Slough, Gwynneth lifted off from a ledge at the Ring of Sacred Volcanoes. Her harvest of bonk coals had been excellent. She had stayed through a full moon. But she was obsessed by the terrible scene she had witnessed on the ridge. The sounds of that *malcadh*'s terrified screams and the image of that torn little body haunted Gwynneth. It seemed like a scene from the darkest realms of hagsmire. Had Hamish, the old Fengo of the Watch, been there, she would have discussed it with him. But there was a new Fengo now, a wolf named Finbar, and she did not feel as close to him.

I suppose, Gwynneth thought, *I could visit the Sark of the Slough.* Gwynneth was an owl—an owl with bonk coals. The Sark loved coals. Both Gwynneth and her father before her father had traded with the Sark. Some said she got along better with owls than she did with her own kind.

The Sark was just removing pots from her kiln when Gwynneth landed. "I have some very good bonk coals for you, ma'am." Owls called the Sark ma'am when addressing her. She seemed to like it. If she hadn't, she would certainly have let them know.

"Any lesser-grade ones?"

"Lesser grades. Why would you want them?"

The Sark turned her head and looked slyly at Gwynneth. "I know conventional wisdom, at least from a collier's or Rogue smith's point of view, is that hotter is better. But you, my dear Gwynneth, deal in metals. I deal in earth, clay, glazes—glazes made from crushed bones, sand, borax, and any mineral I can pull from the river and grind down. But the real secret is not the recipe for the glaze but to fire it at just the right temperature. And to get the right temperature, guess what the secret ingredient is?"

"What?"

"Scat."

"Scat?"

"You call it poop."

"You mean like white splatters, wet poopers?" Gwynneth was shocked. Owls were proud of their neat system of digestion; indeed some felt compelled to call it a noble process.

"Sometimes, but those white splatters—the seagulls especially—are too far away for me." The Sark bent down and kicked a pile of dried moose poop toward Gwynneth.

"Eeew!"

"Don't eeew me. Owls can't smell worth scat—pardon the pun!" The Sark began to mold moose scat into little rounds. "These little moose patties burn steady, burn slow. I can get the most gorgeous glazes you've ever seen." She paused and looked up. The skittering eye was bouncing around as if it had a life of its own, but the other eye was steady as the Sark took in Gwynneth's expression. "Hey, what's wrong with you?"

"What do you mean?"

"You look sick, sick like…no, not the yarpie barpies. Isn't that what you call it when your pellets go soft on you?" The Sark didn't wait for an answer but regarded the Masked Owl with a renewed intensity.

Great Glaux, Gwynneth thought, *how could she tell?* This really was a wolf wise in the way few were. Not that the other wolves were dumb, but the Sark was like one of the healers at the great tree, to whom owls came when they were seriously ill. Well, there was no use trying to hide anything. Gwynneth had to talk to the Sark about what she had found on the ridge. It would be a relief. A pellet seemed to fly up from her gizzard.

"Oh, pardon me, ma'am. I didn't mean to yarp right here!"

"Don't be ridiculous!" replied the Sark. She picked up the pellet in her mouth and plopped it on top of the moose patty. "You don't mind, do you?"

"Mind what?"

"Me using your pellet. I have a hunch this combination could be—how should I put it?—quite dynamic in the kiln. You don't know how long I have been trying to get a turquoise matte glaze."

Gwynneth had no idea what the Sark was talking about. But there was one thing that both Gwynneth and the Sark had in common: They were both artists. "Sure, help yourself," she said.

After the Sark had put the moose patty and the pellet in the kiln, she turned back to Gwynneth. "Well, now that you've yarped your pellet and are looking a tad better, come on inside and tell me what's on your mind."

Gwynneth took a deep breath.

"I'm here about — a *malcadh*."

"You don't say..." The Sark turned around from fluffing a pelt she had dragged nearer to the fire for Gwynneth. The skittish eye grew still. "Why would an owl be interested in a *malcadh*, except of course for the obvious?"

Gwynneth's feathers puffed up with indignation at this last remark. "Because a wolf was interested in that *malcadh* before any owl, fox, cougar, or moose," she snapped.

The hackles of the Sark's fur rose up in a small cyclonic flurry. "What are you saying? The mother came back?"

"No, not the mother. And the pup was not prey for any other animals. It was not eaten."

"Are you saying that..." The Sark gasped and seemed unable to go on.

"Yes. The *malcadh* was murdered."

The Sark's skittish eye went into a spinning frenzy, and her legs began to wobble. "You can't be serious!" But even as she spoke, she knew that this Masked Owl was telling the truth. For a *malcadh*'s life to end this way — it was not a natural death.

"I have never in all my long years…" The Sark's breath came fast and she eased herself onto the heap of rabbit pelts. "All right, tell me what you saw, what you heard." She knew well the extraordinary information that owls could gather through their ear slits. "Tell me everything."

And so Gwynneth did. The fire had begun to gutter out when the Sark finally got up to get some more kindling.

"Are you sure you don't want a bonk coal?" Gwynneth offered, simply to break the long silence with which the Sark had greeted her story.

"No," the Sark growled. "Why waste a good bonk coal on a hearth fire? I have fur, remember. I don't need such a hot fire in my cave."

After tending the fire, she settled down again. "This is very bad, very bad indeed. And you have no idea who this wolf might be?"

"None. That's why I'm here. I thought you might know."

"The only wolf, or kind of wolf, I can imagine doing this might be a foaming-mouth one. You didn't pick up any scent? Oh, I forgot. You can't smell."

"Right. But it might have been an outclanner from the Outermost."

"The clans would have known about it. There is an alert system." The Sark buried her muzzle between her paws. *Why? Why would a wolf do such a thing?* The Sark remained still for several minutes. Finally, she pulled her muzzle out from her paws and said, "So you are the only one who knows about this heinous crime?"

"Well, I suppose so. I mean, I flew off. Someone else could have come along and found...found"—Gwynneth stumbled—"the remains, but they wouldn't know it was a wolf who murdered the *malcadh*. As I told you, I was flying overhead when it happened. I picked up the panting of a wolf, the gnashing of its teeth."

"Huh! So our teeth make that distinctive a sound, do they?"

"Well, for our ears, yes. First of all, as you know, we owls don't have teeth. It's all talons and beaks with us. Fox teeth are much tinier than wolf teeth, and make a scraping sound. Cougars' teeth are huge. They make loud, cracking noises."

"And what about wolf teeth?"

"It's your back teeth that have a unique sound. They slice, sharply. It's not really all that loud—just a clean slicing sound as if two blades are swiping against each other."

The Sark opened her mouth wide and revealed the formidable scissorlike teeth in the back near her throat.

"Yes, quite impressive," Gwynneth said, and averted her eyes with a sudden twist of her head.

The Sark closed her mouth. "So we can safely assume that no other creature except for us knows about this terrible murder."

Gwynneth nodded.

"I think, then, we must keep it that way. I'm going to have to think about this for a while. Describe to me the exact site. Maybe I can go there and pick up a scent."

When Gwynneth finished pinpointing the location on a map she had scratched in the cave floor, the Sark felt there was one scent they would pick up. That of Faolan. For the place was exactly where he had described finding the *malcadh* pup whose mother had recovered in the Sark's cave.

"Faolan was at that ridge," the Sark said casually.

"Surely you're not suggesting Faolan could have done this!" Gwynneth was shocked.

"Oh, no, never. He saw the pup, however. At least a day and a night before you saw it on your flight to the Sacred Ring. But he was in a complete dither when he came here. You can imagine what it was like for a *malcadh* to see another laid out on a *tummfraw*, knowing that he had gone through the same thing. Went straight to his marrow."

"Yes, of course," Gwynneth said, her voice trembling slightly. She sighed. "If you could fly and I could smell, what a team we'd make!"

The Sark blinked several times. She felt her skittish eye still for a moment. "But we can!" she said suddenly.

"Can what? You can't fly. I have no sense of smell. You told me so yourself."

"But don't you see that together we have it all? We might be able to solve this monstrous crime. We are more than the sum of our parts!"

So together the wolf and the owl started to devise a plan in which they would both go to the *tummfraw* on the ridge. They would uncover what clues they could — bones, perhaps tufts of fur that had stuck in small crevices.

"You see, there is — how should I explain it? — a map of scents surrounding everything. You just have to know how to sort them out." The Sark spoke excitedly. Her eye was whirling now. "So I pick up the scent and then try and figure out the direction it came from."

"A vector—a scent vector!" Gwynneth replied. Owls were extraordinary navigators. So they often spoke in terms of navigation when they took bearings on stars or scanned for sound sources.

"Exactly! You see what I mean. We are more than the sum of our parts!"

And at just that moment, the old wolf's nostrils began to twitch. The wind had shifted and on it a vaguely familiar scent wafted into her cave. Indeed, an alarming scent.

"Owl!" she rasped. "You have to go. Visitors are coming and it's best I be alone. Come back two nights from now."

Gwynneth knew better than to argue. She left at once.

CHAPTER EIGHTEEN

A STANDOFF AT THE SCRAPE

THERE WERE IN ALL SIX GNAW wolves who would be competing at the *gaddergnaw* during the Moon of the Singing Grass. They had gathered to practice on the lower slopes of Crooked Back Ridge, a place accessible to all the packs and clans. This morning, the gnaw wolves were working on bones in a gnaw circle that formed around a scrape, a small circular area that had been literally scraped bare of any grass. In the center was a pile of bones from which the wolves selected the ones they wanted. As they gnawed, they spoke softly—clan gossip, the upcoming trials of the big *gaddergnaw*, as well as what they knew of the history of the Ring of Sacred Volcanoes and the wolves of the Watch.

"There's a rumor of outclanners slipping over the

border," Tearlach, the earless gnaw wolf from the MacAngus clan, said. "Have you heard about that?"

"Where — near here?" Edme, the one-eyed wolf from the MacHeath clan, asked nervously.

"Probably not," Heep said. "You know there are always rumors, and if in fact any outclanners are around, most likely they are up near the MacDonegal territory. That's closest to the Outermost border."

"Not a pleasant subject," Edme said, and gave a shiver.

"You know," Tearlach began, as if to purposely change the subject, "they say that when the old Fengo Hamish was released from his duties, his hind leg, which was twisted backward, turned around. A cloud passed across the moon, and when it cleared, his leg was straight."

"Really?" Edme asked somewhat breathlessly.

"But it most certainly is true!" Heep snapped. "Why would you ever question this story?"

"I thought maybe it was just a legend."

"No!" barked Heep. There was a snarl embedded in the bark that took them all aback.

But Edme seemed unfazed. "I don't think we should even think about that because it would mean the good king Soren of the Great Ga'Hoole Tree would have to die, and another owl would have to dive for the ember."

"I never have understood this at all. Embered kings, unembered ones," Faolan said.

"That's because you're new." Heep lifted his head. "You really don't understand our history or our ways."

Faolan went back to his gnawing. He was not going to let this wolf get to him.

"But we should tell him, Heep! Or how will he ever learn?" Creakle, who was missing a paw, leaned out to explain. "As you know, the duty of the Watch is to guard the Ember of Hoole embedded in one of the craters of the five Sacred Volcanoes. That's when there is what we call an unembered monarch such as Soren at the great tree. Embered monarchs have the ember with them, so there's no need for a Watch to guard it.

"What happened to Hamish could happen only after the Ember of Hoole was recovered by Coryn, who became an embered king a long time ago. At that moment, every wolf of the Watch was released from duty and could resume the life of a normal wolf. What had been broken in their bodies was mended; what was twisted was made to grow straight; what was crippled gained strength."

"Is that what the law says?" Faolan asked.

Heep snorted as if to say, *How could one be so stupid?*

but Creakle shot him a dark look. "Oh, no. This was not a decree from the *gaddernock*. It has nothing to do with wolf codes or laws. It was a prophecy." He spoke in a hushed tone. "A prophecy made by the very earliest owl king of the Hoolian world."

"But it came true!" Edme said.

Hasn't it in some way already come true? Faolan thought. He remembered his amazement at the beautiful howling that issued from the throat of the Whistler and wondered again how that buckled throat, the warped windpipe that gusted and rattled in speech, could produce such a lovely note. He said nothing. However, the story of the wolves of the Watch being restored to new lives had a haunting resonance for him.

The wolves at the scrape were silent for a long time after Creakle's explanation. Faolan liked this new companionship but was deeply annoyed that he had to gnaw so close to Heep. He could almost hear that little nick in the back blades of Heep's teeth clicking as he gnawed. Wolves of the same clan had to work next to each other. This meant that Heep, the Whistler, and Faolan always had to gnaw side by side.

Across the scrape from Faolan were Creakle the MacDuff wolf, Tearlach from the MacAngus clan, and Edme, the pathetic one-eyed she-wolf who had endured unspeakable abuse from the infamous MacHeath clan. One of the vilest secrets of the MacHeaths was that they would purposely maim young pups, hoping to gain a place in the Watch of the Sacred Volcanoes. MacDuncans had been favored for the Watch, but when Hamish became Fengo, he worked hard with the best scholars of the *gaddernock* so that the law could be changed and others could be considered for duty. Hamish felt that new blood was needed to keep the Watch vigorous. It had been one of his last achievements before he died.

As they chatted and gnawed around the scrape, Faolan worked on a design that he hoped someday to perfect so he could carve it on Thunderheart's huge paw. It was a carving of a summer night when Thunderheart had watched the stars with Faolan, naming the constellations for him and pointing out the Great Bear. Faolan was determined to incise this constellation on his bone— every little star from the Bear's muzzle to the tips of its hind feet.

Edme had risen up to stretch her legs. "Oh, my goodness! Look at what Faolan's done!" she exclaimed.

"What?" grunted Heep.

"Why, he's only made the most beautiful constellation I have ever seen. With all the proper stars surrounding it."

"It looks like a bear, not a wolf—if that's what you intended." Heep scowled.

"That's exactly what I intended. It is how the bears look at the stars. They call the Great Wolf the Great Bear. My second Milk Giver taught me those names. The Great Bear points to Ursulana, the place where bear spirits go when they die."

"Oh, her again, that bear," muttered Heep.

"It's beautiful, Heep!" Edme said. "What difference does it make what one calls it? Stars all have different meaning for different animals, and heavens have different names. It's an inspiration." She scurried to the center of the circle and picked a femur from the pile, then returned to her spot and began gnawing diligently. "I'm starting over, a new bone, new design! All because of Faolan!"

Edme was such a cheerful wolf despite her pitiful appearance.

"Yes, Faolan's is one of the loveliest designs ever." The windy words of the Whistler brushed Faolan's shoulder as Whistler leaned over to study the bone. "Edme's right; what difference does it make?"

"Blasphemy, perhaps?" Heep muttered.

"I think you're going too far," Creakle said.

"That's your opinion, Creakle. But some might call it

profane to call the Great Wolf by the name of another animal."

"Oh, really!" The Whistler groaned and it sounded like the clattering of bare branches in the wind.

Faolan knew that his gnawing had caused talk, especially since he had gnawed the bones of contrition. The elegance and beauty of his work had stirred rumors among the most superstitious of the wolves that he was from the Dim World, or perhaps was the *malcadh* offspring of an outclanner! Wolves were watching him closely now, and it was unnerving. If Heep began muttering about the constellation he had just carved and saying it was blasphemy, there could be trouble. But should Faolan change his design to look more like a wolf? That seemed dishonest, even profane. He had wanted to show how bears viewed the night sky. The bear's point of view. Did the entire universe always have to be seen through the eyes of wolves?

Edme paused in her gnawing. "Don't you find it odd that both wolves and cougars share the word 'scrape,' but the meaning is so different?"

The clicking sound next to Faolan stopped. Heep dropped his bone. He began to make the writhing motions that often were the prelude to one of his humble speeches. "I am well aware that I am the humblest of all the gnaw wolves gathered here today, and perhaps I am reaching beyond my lowly station to even suggest that the esteemed gnaw wolf from the MacHeath clan goes too far."

Faolan felt his hackles rise at this. Heep had just wrapped an insult in the deceptive pelt of his fawning words. Poor Edme knew that she was the least-esteemed gnaw wolf in all the Beyond because the brutal clan she came from was a whisker's breadth away from being considered outclanners. Heep's words rubbed a raw wound.

"But it is my humble opinion that it does a disservice to our noble wolves to even think of a comparison between our clans and cougars." And with that, Heep got up, walked around to where Edme was working, and gave her a sharp nip on the ear.

"*Youch!*" Edme screeched. A trickle of blood ran down her neck.

The other wolves were momentarily stunned. Tearlach was at Edme's side instantly, and the other wolves soon jumped up, their hackles raised.

"Are you all right, Edme?" Tearlach asked.

"I'll be fine. It wasn't deep. I'll be fine." But she did not look fine.

Edme's face seemed to be collapsing into her skull. Her muzzle trembled, her eye leaked oily tears. But she stared at Heep uncomprehendingly. "Why? Why would you do such a thing?"

"You need to learn, Edme. Your comments were an insult to our species."

"I...I..." she began to speak.

She can't apologize. She can't! Faolan thought. He had had enough of the yellow wolf for one morning. He knew it was not so much what Edme had said but her drawing attention to Faolan's carving earlier that had angered Heep. Heep was trying to get back at her. Faolan came right up to Heep and assumed the most threatening posture he could muster, for gnaw wolves were not practiced in the basics of threat stances and dominance signals. And yet the other gnaw wolves dropped their bones when they saw Faolan with his tail erect, his head held high, his ears shoved up and forward.

Faolan circled Heep, walking with a slight swagger until he stopped and faced him. He growled and bared his teeth. Then he began to speak, and what he said was so shocking that the other wolves gasped: "Heep, you are prideful. You are not humble at all. And you are a hypocrite. Pride and deceit have made you mean. What you just said to Edme was cruel. You are vain. Your so-called humility is false. You want to be humiliated? I'll help you!"

And now Faolan did the most extraordinary thing of all. He reared up and placed his two front paws across Heep's shoulders to press him down. This was the most aggressive of all the dominance moves a wolf could make.

This was not a fight; not a drop of blood was shed. But as the four other gnaw wolves watched, they understood that they were seeing something more disturbing than a fight. None of them had any fondness for Heep, but they were frightened by Faolan's display of dominance. It violated every rule and code of the *gaddernock* for a gnaw wolf to use dominance signals.

When Faolan removed his front paws, Heep staggered to his feet and looked around. His eyes were narrow slits. "You made an error, gnaw wolf." The words seemed to seethe through his teeth, but Heep kept his ears flat and would not look Faolan in the eye. "I could report this. It would be the end for you."

The Whistler came forward then and spoke, his thin voice warbling like a wind through a deep canyon. "No, it won't be the end. It's the beginning. And you won't report it, Heep. Trust me on that!" He reared up on his hind legs as well and placed his forepaws on Heep's shoulders. No sooner had he stepped down than Creakle, who was missing a forepaw, stepped up, skewered himself around so his two back paws were squarely on Heep's shoulders, and pressed down as well. The earless Tearlach was next, and finally Edme came forward.

Her single eye was an intense deep green that seemed to sparkle with unshed tears. Before she reared up, she spoke in her high, distinct little voice. "You hurt me, Heep. Not the nip to my ear—that was nothing. The way you spoke was cruel. Believe me, I know cruel. I come from the MacHeath clan. We may be gnaw wolves here at the scrape, but we are civilized. You are an uncivilized wolf, Heep."

When she stepped off Heep's shoulders, the Whistler came forward again. "And now, Heep, you are truly humiliated. Do us the favor of not expanding on your humiliation."

Faolan was deeply touched by the loyalty of the other gnaw wolves. And he should have slept well, but his dreams were troubled once more by the tale of the *skreeleen* and the little pup who kept trying to go back down the star ladder. The images of that little pup mixed with the loathsome clicking sounds from Heep's teeth. Why couldn't Faolan put this to rest? How many more bones did he need to find?

He had been back once and found more, which he had also taken to bury with the paw of Thunderheart. The grizzly had been his mother in life; she could watch over the little pup in death. After all, she knew pups. She had raised Faolan not just on her milk, but had taught him to hunt and to jump! Perhaps she could help this pup jump for the star ladder.

But every time he thought of the little *malcadh*, he thought of the story of Skaarsgard chasing after the stubborn star pup who scampered down the star ladder so he could taste the meat of the fox and swim the river to fish for salmon. Who could have no dreams because he had not lived. Once more, Faolan felt deep in his marrow that it was not dreams the little she-pup on the ridge came back for, not ox, not salmon, but vengeance.

CHAPTER NINETEEN

THE BONE TURNS

HEEP HAD LEFT THE SCRAPE SHAKING with rage. Rage and fear. He had been wary of Faolan since the very first day, when the wolf had jumped the wall of fire. Rumors had begun about Faolan challenging the order and had trailed Faolan ever since. Everything had been going so well until now. Faolan's extravagant display of pride during the *byrrgis* three moons before could not have worked better for Heep. But now somehow, as the old wolf expression went, the bone had turned, and Heep was denounced as the prideful gnaw wolf. But that bone Faolan had incised at the scrape was a profanity! Imagine carving a design of the most important constellation in the night sky and making it look like a bear! This was challenging the order, and Heep would make sure word leaked out about it. The clans, particularly the MacDuffs, were already deeply suspicious of Faolan. Perhaps what transpired at the scrape had happened for the best.

Heep had spent his life feeling desperately sorry for himself. Of all the afflictions gnaw wolves suffered—missing eyes, paws, crooked throats—his was the worst. There was nothing that compared with the indignity of not having a tail.

The tail was the most expressive part of a wolf's body. To hold it high and wave it indicated confidence, happiness, and dominance within a pack. Held rigid and straight out, it was a clear signal of aggression and impending attack. The tail half-tucked was a sign of submission, and fully tucked meant the wolf was afraid. Heep, whose entire life had been dedicated to humility, did not even have the most important instrument of all to show how humble he was. That was what perhaps galled him the most.

It was all so unfair. Sometimes he wondered if it would have been better if he'd died on his *tummfraw*. But when he saw this new wolf violating every single rule of the *byrrgis*, how could he help feeling superior, even without a tail?

It was now the deepest part of a moonless night,

and Heep heard Faolan stirring. Was that foul wolf going roaming again? One would think that the splayed paw would make more of a track, especially on rainy nights. But the silver wolf was crafty, and Heep believed that Faolan had figured out a way to camouflage his paw print. He was a hard wolf to follow and he traveled so fast. Again, Heep's mind went back to how it was all so unfair that he had been born without a tail. Even a wolf born *malcadh* because of his strange paw could devise a strategy to hide his deformity. But what could Heep do without a tail? Grow one? Nothing short of a miracle would make that happen.

Heep got up and silently made his way out of the *gaddergnaw* camp. He would try to follow Faolan. The night was dark, but that silvery tail waved like a pennant in the blackness.

It had been a long night and taken twice as long as Faolan had planned to travel to the ridge of the pup, as he now thought of that sad, bleak place. At first, Faolan had felt as if he were being followed and had taken several detours that added greatly to the journey. But he found some more of the little pup's bones and then traveled fast to Thunderheart's paw. He looked forward to the breaking dawn, when gray would start to peel back the dark of the moonless night.

A northeast wind had begun and brought in a wet, foggy mist. Soon it was drizzling. Faolan peered down at the bones before he buried them, his forehead wrinkling as he scrutinized the marks.

Violence. That was all he could imagine. Wanton violence seemed to seep from the bones and their helter-skelter flurry of teeth incisions. What animal would have done this? How could an animal be *angry* at its prey? Prey was a fact of life; there was no need or reason for passion. A defenseless animal like the little she-pup could not have put up a fight. Why this madness?

Faolan dug down and tucked the *malcadh*'s bones in so they nestled close to Thunderheart. He then turned north and headed back toward the Eastern Scree. The *gaddergnaw* gathering on the western slopes of Crooked Back Ridge would have disbanded by now and the packs gone back to their own camps. The fog had thickened, but Faolan knew his way and found it comforting to be wrapped in the vaporous ground mist. Insulated, protected in his downy pelt still thick with winter fur, he was alone with his thoughts and indulged in his dreams of Thunderheart and the pup climbing the star ladder together. In Faolan's waking dreams, the pup never fell off the ladder and never ever tried to scramble back down to earth.

CHAPTER TWENTY

THE SARK'S VISITOR

THE SARK THOUGHT SHE HAD LIVED so long that nothing would astonish her, but now she was staggering in her own den with disbelief. She had experienced two astounding revelations in one day. The first was the murder of the *malcadh*, and the second was the appearance in her own den of Faolan's mother! She connected the scent of the she-wolf almost immediately to the amazing wolf who had jumped the wall of fire. Morag and her second mate had come from the MacDonegal clan far to the northwest.

Only a wolf with the Sark's exceptional powers of scent detection would have decoded the odors that linked Morag with her long-lost son. It was impossible — at least the Sark believed it to be impossible — that Faolan's mother would remember the scent of a son born two years ago. Yet Morag seemed nervous and kept sniffing the place where Faolan had curled up.

"A lot of wolves come to you?" Morag asked, a tinge of suspicion in her voice.

"A few."

"Do you think you might help her?" Brangwen asked.

"It's hard to tell. Come over here to the other side of the fire, dear." The Sark wanted to get Morag away from Faolan's spot. Her paws shook as she rolled the compresses of borage and shredded birch bark. "Now, I am making you up some compresses that need to soak in the river before you apply them. You can make them yourself when these are finished. Just borage and shredded birch bark. If there isn't any borage about, use mosses. You needn't even soak them if you use the mosses." Her voice was shaking. She hoped they wouldn't notice, but of course they had never visited before and might think this was her normal way of speaking.

"And if it doesn't work?" Brangwen pressed.

What am I supposed to say to that? she thought. *If it doesn't work, she goes blind. She won't be able to hunt. She'll become a burden to her pack, her clan. Their share of the meat will diminish.* It was obvious to the Sark that this she-wolf had been a great hunter. Probably a great outflanker. She had massive shoulders and powerful back legs. Now, because of her failing eyesight, every step she took was tentative. She seemed even more feeble than she actually was. It was odd with wolves that went blind. They could be perfectly healthy in every other respect, but when their vision began to go, they were forced to engage with their surroundings in an entirely new way. They moved much more slowly, more cautiously. As the world around them faded, they began to withdraw. Their very muscles seemed to contract, and the wolves receded into themselves, occupying an inner landscape until only a brittle shell was left of the wolf that had once existed. It was a kind of living death, a retreat of the body and a contraction of the spirit.

"If it doesn't work—" The Sark sighed. "These are questions I cannot answer. But if it doesn't work, perhaps you should consider joining the MacNamara clan. As you have probably heard, they are very tolerant of females who have served well but have become old before their time."

"But that is so far," Brangwen said.

Morag remained silent. She did not stir. It was as if she were already far away.

The Sark watched as Morag and Brangwen wound down the narrow, twisting path that led away from her camp. She shoved more moose patties into her kiln and then went back into the cave for the memory jug that contained the scraps of her recollections of Faolan — from the first time she saw the splayed paw print that led to his jump for the sun to his most recent visit. She pressed her muzzle into the throat of the jug and began to whisper.

"On this day, the last of the winter moons, there came to my den the she-wolf Morag, mother of Faolan the *malcadh*, mate now of Brangwen and member of the MacDonegal clan. I fear she might have picked up a trace of her son's scent. She is a strong wolf, deep of chest, with powerful haunches. I would guess an outflanker, but her days of running the *byrrgis* are over. She suffers from the milk-eye disease and, I fear, will soon be blind. May Lupus watch over her until she climbs the star ladder."

The Sark walked from her den and looked up, scanning the sky for Gwynneth.

CHAPTER TWENTY-ONE

THE STRANGER

FAOLAN HAD LOST TRACK OF THE number of trips and the number of bones he had retrieved from the ridge. And yet he was as frustrated as ever. He simply did not understand how the little pup could have met such an unconscionable death. Until things became clearer, Faolan was hesitant to build the *drumlyn* he had planned for the she-pup. He did not want to disturb the bones further by gnawing through that white squall of marks to tell the short story of the pup who died dreamless on the ridge. So each time he found a bone, he dutifully took it to be buried in Thunderheart's paw. As long as they were within those clawtips, he felt the grizzly would keep them safe.

Shortly after Faolan left the ridge, two other animals of the Beyond began to comb the slope just below the *tummfraw.* Gwynneth hovered annoyingly close above the Sark as the wolf sniffed the rocky terrain.

"Would you give me a bit of space here?! There's hardly enough air for us to breathe, let alone for me to pick up a scent," the Sark snapped.

"Sorry!" Gwynneth replied.

"Remember what I told you. You've got the eyes. I've got the sniffer. You should be flying well above me, trying to spot bones in the runoffs down this slope. I'll try to pick up a scent."

"Yes, of course," Gwynneth said. The Sark knew, however, that Gwynneth couldn't resist hovering and would be back shortly. But the Sark herself was stymied. She felt as if she were trapped in a web of scents. It had been easy to pick up the *malcadh*'s scent. After all, the pup's mother had been in the Sark's den for two days and three nights. Faolan had arrived soon after the mother, and he, too, bore the scent of a live pup. But mingled with those three base scents of the pup, the mother, and Faolan were other odors, similar yet distinct, that seemed hopelessly entangled. A moose had passed this way, as had a cougar. But another wolfish scent was buried beneath all that. Possibly from the MacDuncan clan, but then again, it might have been a MacDuff wolf. As to which pack in which clan — that would be even harder to determine after all these moons. And finally, overlaying all these odors was the fresher scent of Faolan, who had visited this *tummfraw* many times. Curious! All the scents were layered in a vaguely chronological order and yet at the same time scrambled in a manner that made no sense to the Sark. The one thing she knew for certain was that, when Faolan had arrived at her cave, he had borne with him the odor of a live pup, and it was while Faolan was still at the cave that Gwynneth had witnessed the brutal attack. By the time she had landed, the pup was dead and the wolf had vanished.

"I've got something! I've got something!" Gwynneth swooped down with a tiny rib in her talons. She dropped it in front of the Sark's paws.

The Sark bent down and nudged it gently with her muzzle. "What you have here, my dear Gwynneth, is the bone of a very young pup, perhaps two days old."

"Yes, the pup. The *malcadh*!"

"Really, you exceed yourself. Indeed, these surpass my own minor achievements. Although your thinking is not what one would call radiant, you can on occasion be a reflection of light." The Sark peered into Gwynneth's jet-black eyes. Masked Owls were among the few species that had black eyes as opposed to yellow or amber-colored ones.

Gwynneth was beginning to feel that this conversation was becoming less than complimentary. She was right. The Sark was slightly miffed that Gwynneth had come up with the first clear evidence of the victim.

"Some creatures," the Sark continued, "although not brilliant themselves, have a remarkable capacity for simulating it." When the Sark became miffed, she could become rather intellectually pompous.

"Am I supposed to thank you for telling me that I am not so bright?" Gwynneth replied in even tones.

The Sark was instantly taken aback. "I'm sorry." Her bad eye began to skitter. "I was unkind. You have brought me a good bone. And look at these marks — an unintelligible blizzard that speaks only of violence and murder and supports what you heard. *Why* we must ask ourselves. Perhaps that is a more important question than this confounding tangle of scents." The Sark peered down at the bone. "By method of exclusion, we can eliminate Faolan. He was with me in the cave at the time of the murder. So he could not be the culprit. We do know it is a wolf, for you, with your excellent auditory skills, heard the panting. These teeth marks support that it was a wolf and they cut deeply, deeper than a fox's teeth yet not with the distinctive slashing of a cougar. The scent marks are too scrambled for me to figure out much. So far" — she began to scratch some lines on the ground—"I can detect five different wolf scents."

"Five!" Gwynneth found this staggering.

"Yes, five. Some are direct lay-downs, as I call them. Others are indirect, or what we might term remote, scents picked up by association with one of the main players. The pup, of course, is a direct lay-down, as is the Obea's scent, as well as Faolan's. But mixed in with these three is at least one other, possibly two. One is a direct lay-down, presumably from the murderer, but the other is indirect, I am fairly sure. The problem is that these two other scents are hopelessly intertwined."

"So you can't sort out which is the murderer's and which is not."

"Exactly."

"One could be an accomplice," Gwynneth offered.

"True! True." New light twinkled in the Sark's good eye.

Please don't call me a conductor of light! Gwynneth thought.

"I must give the notion of an accomplice, perhaps a remote accomplice, more thought," said the Sark.

CHAPTER TWENTY-TWO

THE GADDERGNAW
GAMES BEGIN!

MOST OF THE BEYOND WAS BARREN.
Ice-pruned over thousands of years, the land grew few
true forests. The soil, poor and thin, could not support
much vegetation. But to the south, near the borders of
the Hoolian kingdoms, there were vast expanses of grass-
lands. It was true, Faolan thought, the grass did sing as
the dry southeast wind blew through it. But the singing
grass was lost now in the barking and howling of the *gaddergludder* in anticipation of the Gaddergnaw Games. All
the packs of all the clans, even if they did not have a
gnaw wolf, attended the *gaddergnaw*. There were festivi-
ties, howling by the *skreeleens*, lively and sometimes
acrimonious debates on various finer points of the *gaddernock*. And this all happened before the competitions even
started. The most dramatic moment of the *gaddergnaw*,

almost more exciting in many ways than the announcement of the games winner who would go on to serve in the Watch, was the arrival of the Fengo and the *taigas* from the Ring of Sacred Volcanoes.

Faolan and the Whistler had just been trotting over to the bone piles to select their bones for the first event, when Mhairie stepped out from behind one of the mounds.

"There are some awfully good femurs over there in that stack." She nodded toward a mound that was not nearly as high as the others. "I know the pile looks picked over, but it hasn't been." Neither Faolan nor the Whistler nor any of the other gnaw wolves could get used to the new deference and respect shown to them by the other wolves. But it was only temporary. Once the games finished, it was life as usual for the gnaw wolves not selected. Faolan simply could not imagine going on forever as a gnaw wolf. But he had no way of gauging his chances. He might have skills that were valued by the wolves of the Watch, but there were so many rumors swirling about him. He had challenged the order, and now he heard whispers about his "profane" carving of the Great Bear constellation. Heep had been effective in getting the word out about that. Faolan was glad he had not changed his design, but he had no idea if his odd and beautiful carving would hurt or help his bid for the Watch.

"Let's get over there before anybody else does!" The Whistler trotted off, with Faolan behind him.

"Can you wait up a moment, Faolan?" Mhairie asked.

"Uh, sure."

"I...I..." Mhairie stammered. "I just wanted to wish you luck in the contests. And you know I'm sure you'll do wonderfully in the *byrrgis*. You can run full out. You get to run in the sublieutenant positions—as a packer or a line wolf. But sometimes packers bump up against the captains. It takes a great deal of experience not to. Happens all the time. So don't worry about it."

"When it does happen, it's not a violation of the *byrrgnock*, I suppose." It was not a question. Faolan said this in a flat voice.

"No, why would it be?"

"Of course not. There aren't gnaw wolves running in these positions in normal *byrrgises*. Why waste abuse on some wolf who isn't a gnaw wolf?"

"I don't think you understand what I am saying, Faolan. You won't be punished if it does happen."

"I understand perfectly. I won't be abused this time because this is a special *byrrgis*. But if I fail to be selected and return to pack life, the rules of the game change back."

"I suppose so," Mhairie said. She seemed suddenly nervous.

"Did you have something else to say, Mhairie?"

"I do." She paused and looked directly into his eyes. "Faolan, there are some rumors going around the encampment."

"What kind of rumors?"

"About a bone you carved at a practice session around the time of the Moon of the Cracking Ice. Some say it was..." Her eyes shifted down to the ground.

"Profane?"

"Yes." She swung her eyes toward him again. Her hackles raised and seemed to quiver.

"I carved a constellation. I carved the Great Wolf only from the point of view of my second Milk Giver."

"The grizzly?"

"Yes. She was the first one who told me about the star pictures. She and the others of her kind call it the Great Bear."

Mhairie cocked her head. "That's very interesting."

"Yes, Mhairie, it is interesting, but it's not profane."

"Not in the least," Mhairie agreed. "But still be careful."

A passel of young pups went tumbling by, chasing one another.

"Time out! Time out!" one pure-white pup said, skidding to a halt. "I don't want to play tag anymore. Let's play go-to-the-Sark."

Mhairie turned to the pups. "That's a stupid game," she muttered, and began to walk away.

But Faolan was riveted. The white pup was obviously the boss of this gang. She turned to a brindled pup whose pale brown fur had patches of gray and black. "You'll be the Sark."

"But I'm a male."

"It doesn't matter," the white pup snapped.

"You be the Obea," she said, turning to another pup whose fur was the color of a storm cloud.

"They stink," whined the pup.

"No, that's the problem. They don't stink at all. They have no scent. Now quit complaining. It's just a play. And, Bryan," she said to another wolf, who was also white and most likely her brother. "You be the *malcadh*. You can tuck your back leg behind you and walk on three like we've been practicing."

"Sure," said the white pup in a voice of resignation, as if he was used to being bossed by this older sibling.

"And I am the mother." She immediately threw herself onto the ground and began to sob. "Don't take my pup!" More sobs. "This is my last litter. I promise I shall have no more. Leave me my last daughter!"

"I'm not a daughter," the white pup complained. "I'm a son."

"For the play, you're a daughter. Now just shut your muzzle."

Then the pup playing the Obea spoke sternly, "I must take this *malcadh* to the *tummfraw*. You need to go to the Sark and begin the forgetting. She will brew you a potion." The pup playing the mother swung her head toward the brindled pup and whispered loudly, "Start mixing up a potion!"

"I don't have anything to mix. There aren't any herbs or grass or leaves or even birch bark."

"Just mix up some dirt and stones. It's all make-believe." She turned to another pup. "Now when the *malcadh* survives and comes back to the clan, you can start kicking him and nipping his ear. But you know, just pretend."

Faolan watched all of this mesmerized. *Just pretend! This is my life! They are playacting with my life.* He was about to say something, but he didn't know what. Surely a gnaw wolf could not reprimand young pups.

Mhairie stepped from behind a rock. "This isn't the time for make-believe," she said sternly.

"Why not?" challenged the white pup. "Just because you're bigger and you say so?"

"No," Mhairie said quietly. "Because this is a gnaw wolf." She nodded at Faolan. "And his life is real, not make-believe. There is no just-pretending when he is bitten and kicked."

The pups all grew very still. Then the white one stepped forward. "You're absolutely the hugest wolf I've ever seen! And you're the gnaw wolf who jumped for the sun, aren't you? They said you disturbed the order."

"I didn't jump for the sun. I jumped for my life." Faolan stood straighter, squared his shoulders, and lifted his tail just a bit. In the evening light, he was bright and silvery, and the pups once again fell silent, for they had never seen a young wolf with such noble bearing. And to think he was a gnaw wolf!

Suddenly, a howl peeled through the air. It was Alastrine, *skreeleen* of the MacDuncan Carreg Gaer. Soon, other *skreeleens* joined in. Barks and yips from all the clans scored the air.

"They're coming! They're coming! The Fengo Finbar and the *taigas* are coming!"

"Come on," Mhairie said. "I know a good place to watch from."

Faolan followed Mhairie as she scrambled up an escarpment. Soon, another wolf joined them. "This is my sister Dearlea," Mhairie said, looking over her shoulder as they made their way up the steep slope. Dearlea was a deep brown that perhaps had once been lighter, like her sister's tawny gold, but despite their difference in color, there was a strong resemblance.

"Oh, look!" Dearlea exclaimed as they reached the top. There was a long line of wolves wending their way down a narrow defile.

"Can you hear the *tinulaba?*" Mhairie asked.

"What?" said Faolan.

Mhairie and Dearlea looked at each other in dismay.

"You don't know what the *tinulaba* is?" Dearlea asked.

"No."

"The *tinulaba* is the clinking sound tailbones make when they jingle-jangle against one another softly. That's what the word means—'chimes of the bones.' The wolves of the Watch make their necklaces out of those small little bones from the tails of animals."

"They wear necklaces? I thought only the clan chieftains and members of the *raghnaid* wore them."

"No, wolves of the Watch can wear them, too. But theirs are made out of just the tailbones. They gnaw them."

"They gnaw designs into tailbones?" Faolan was astonished. Tailbones were among the smallest.

"Yes, you'll learn how to do it when—" Mhairie stopped herself. "I mean *if* you are selected for the Watch. The *taigas* will teach you."

All the barking and howling stopped. A silence descended over the land as the wind rose from the direction of the Watch wolves' procession and carried with it the *tinulaba*. The *tinulaba* was not merely a sound but truly music, chimes that went straight to Faolan's marrow and stirred him deeply.

As the Watch wolves slowed on the steepest part of the defile, he could observe them more carefully. They were large, muscular animals. It was often said that a *malcadh*'s deformity could become a source of strength.

Even from a distance, the Watch exuded a power and confidence that Faolan had never seen before.

Of all the wolves, the Fengo was the most elaborately bedecked in bone necklaces. He even had tiny fragments of bone braided into his beard. Mhairie and Dearlea began to whisper.

"There's Jasper," Dearlea said, pointing her muzzle toward a dark brown wolf.

"That's Briar, isn't it?" Mhairie said.

"The red wolf with the bad eye?" Dearlea asked.

"Yes. There are two red wolves, and I always get them mixed up because they both have bad eyes," Mhairie said.

Faolan wondered how they knew so much. They seemed to be able to identify every wolf and his or her particular deformity while the wolves were still a fair distance away.

"And they are sister and brother. That makes it harder," Dearlea replied.

"Sister and brother?" Faolan could not hide his surprise.

"Yes, very unusual. Two *malcadhs* in one litter."

"That must have been nice for them...I mean the pups." Faolan detested the word *malcadh*. "I mean they had company."

"Not so nice for the mother." Dearlea sighed. "Imagine

two of her litter born *malcadhs*. And who knows; maybe she only had two pups that year."

"But they both survived and returned to the clan," Mhairie said. "Imagine that!"

Yes, thought Faolan. *Imagine that!* He looked at the two sister wolves who stood beside him. They were so lucky to have been born whole and perfect and to be sisters. And though he would never wish his life on another, wouldn't it have been easier to have a brother or sister with him on that *tummfraw*?

CHAPTER TWENTY-THREE

GWYNNETH'S ADVICE

THE FIRST EVENT OF THE *GADDERGNAW* was the *byrrgis*. The scouts had gone to look for the first of the caribou herds migrating north. Just past dawn, one came back with news. A small herd had crossed the river and was heading north by northeast at tock-tock speed.

"To the west or east of Crooked Back Ridge?" Liam MacDuncan asked. The large gray wolf had become the chieftain of the clan after his father, Duncan, died. But there were whispers that his mother, Cathmor, was the real power and guided him in every decision.

"They are crimping easterly."

There were barks of approval, for this meant the herd was heading directly into MacDuncan territory.

Cathmor stepped forward. "Don't count on it. The herd could split at the base of the ridge. I think it would be wise if this *byrrgis* of gnaw wolves had experience in pincering. After all, pincer strategies are fundamental to all the *byrrgises* run by the gnaw wolves of the Beyond. Their responsibilities at the Ring of Sacred Volcanoes prohibit them from chasing herds too far. They do not have the luxury of extended hunts as we do. Why not see how these young gnaw wolves do?"

"Pincering?" Tearlach said in a shaky voice. "I've never done a pincer move."

"I must humbly remind you, Tearlach, that none of us has ever been anything but the lowliest sweeper," Heep interjected.

A low scathing hiss issued from the Whistler's throat. "I humbly beg you to go off and eat a moose patty!"

The other gnaw wolves began to chuckle and wag their tails. Despite Tearlach's apprehensions, all the gnaw wolves were excited to be running as truly significant members of the *byrrgis* and not sniffing the prey's scat or urine. This was the one and only time that other wolves took on the responsibilities of sweepers.

"Can you beat that!" Little Edme gave Faolan a gentle poke and tossed her head toward Heep, who had moved off after the Whistler's remarks. Once again, Edme, despite having been born with only one eye, saw everything. The yellow wolf was now prostrating himself and began to writhe excessively before a handsome black wolf from the MacDuff clan, a high-ranking *raghnaid* member.

"What's he saying?" Edme asked.

Faolan shoved his ears forward. But as seemed to be the tendency with gnaw wolves, it was the earless Tearlach who picked up the conversation.

"Dunstan MacDuff, I understand that your esteemed son has agreed to run as a sweeper so that we ignoble gnaw wolves might for this one time assume loftier positions in the *byrrgis*. Although it might seem presumptuous of me, a lowly, humble —"

"Here we go again," said Edme. They had surreptitiously crept a bit closer and could now hear Heep without Tearlach's aid.

"I thought I might offer some modest advice in regard to the sniffing of scat." This was one of Heep's most theatrical displays of humiliation and ingratiation, which was fortunately soon drowned out by the rallying howls of the *gaddergludder*.

Faolan was to be a packer alongside Mhairie's sister Dearlea, who was a tight-end packer on the western flank. Heep was also a packer on the western flank.

Why couldn't they have at least assigned him to the eastern flank? Faolan thought grimly. Why couldn't it have been the Whistler at his side? Why was it always Heep?

Just as they were forming up for the *byrrgis*, Creakle barked, "Look! Owls—a lot of them!" He pointed his muzzle toward the sky.

Dearlea, who was passing by, stopped. "Oh, yes, they love to see *gaddergnaws*. Mostly colliers and Rogue smiths."

I wonder, Faolan thought, *if Gwynneth is here?* At that very moment, the Masked Owl swooped down.

"Oh, Gwynneth, I'm so excited to see you. I've tried to do what you told me to. Become a gnaw wolf."

"Yes, dear, I know."

"I've had some...some..."

"Slipups? Yes, I heard about that first *byrrgis*." Faolan dropped his tail. "Well, I know you've most likely learned your lesson." Gwynneth paused.

It seemed to Faolan there was something else she wanted to say to him. He peered into her shiny dark eyes. "What is it, Gwynneth?"

"It can wait until after the *byrrgis*. We'll talk then."

The summoning howl curled into the air. "To the Marrow!" The *byrrgis* was about to begin.

"I have to go now, Gwynneth."

"I know, dear. All of you gnaw wolves are going to have more responsibility than ever in this *byrrgis*."

"Why's that?"

"Well, an alert has just gone out. Outclanners have been spotted. So some of the scouts and wolves that would normally be in the *byrrgis* are hunting them down. I tried to help a bit as best I could. But the point is, there's more opportunity for you gnaw wolves to show what you're made of. Just one piece of advice."

"What's that?"

"It's not all speed."

"Oh, I've learned my lesson about that. Don't worry! I won't bump an outflanker."

"No, I know that." Gwynneth paused. "Look, I've been flying in the Beyond for longer than I care to remember. I have flown right above *byrrgises* and seen them from a perspective that you, or any other wolf, never will. It's the signaling that counts—a pricked set of ears, a tail twitch, a quick change in pace by the packers. It's not speed. It's communication that makes them flow like a river across dry land and finally engulf their prey. It's about communicating, yet never uttering a word."

CHAPTER TWENTY-FOUR

THE BYRRGIS OF
THE GNAW WOLVES

HEEP KNEW THAT THERE WAS NO
way he could outrun Faolan in a *byrrgis*. But could he out-
wit him? There was one thing that really set Faolan's
nerves on edge. It was the clicking sound Heep's back
teeth made when he gnawed bones. Heep had seen
how it made Faolan's hackles rise. How Faolan could
barely keep his agitation under control. To Heep, his teeth
on the bone sounded no different than that of any other
gnaw wolf, but something bothered Faolan about Heep's
teeth.

Heep didn't need a bone in his mouth to make those
sounds. He could do it without one. Therefore, he was
extremely pleased when he was assigned to the same flank
as Faolan. Heep was in a perfect spot to drive that gnaw
wolf *cag mag*!

They had started off at press paw over the hilly terrain, led by the scouts. It was not long before the caribou herd came into sight. Luckily, the *byrrgis* was downwind, so the caribou would not pick up their scent. This allowed the wolves to get closer before being discovered. The longer they could go at press paw while closing the distance, the better. It conserved their energy and was the most efficient running. Of course, if the wind shifted, their strategy did, too.

Faolan was concentrating as hard as he ever had. At last he was in the *byrrgis*—not as a sweeper, not in a dream, not as a distant observer on a ridge, longing to be a part of the hunt. This was real. The hard earth flew beneath him. He was barely aware of his paws striking the ground except for a tingle that traveled up through his femurs. But he felt a surge of vibrations from hundreds of paws pounding the earth. It washed over him, enveloped him, welded him to this hunt, these packs of wolves. At last he was truly part of something.

Faolan was very grateful that he had spoken to Gwynneth. Her advice was already proving invaluable. He had just picked up a second signal, which had traveled from a line wolf to a wide-end packer, and knew the entire formation of over forty wolves was about to compact itself.

It's like Gwynneth said, he thought, *the* byrrgis *is a river flowing over dry ground. And I am part of it. Like the stars swirling endlessly in the sky, I am part of this river on earth.* For the first time, Faolan began to understand what *hwlyn* meant, and the strange ways of the wolves of the Beyond began to have a deeper meaning. The silent flickers sang through his bloodstream as he raced on.

More signals were passed and the language of silence became clearer and clearer to Faolan. He spotted the ear flick of another wide-end packer. The wind had shifted, and the *byrrgis* immediately increased its speed as the caribou herd caught the wolves' scent.

Close the distance! The signal rang out as crisply as if it had been spoken. Faolan felt the *byrrgis* close up for attack speed.

This is beautiful! Faolan thought. The motions were flawless. It suddenly struck him that this was like *biliboo.* The wolves, like the pieces in the game, floated almost magically across the land, just as the constellations slid across the night sky.

On moonless nights, when the stars shone even brighter in the black infinity, Faolan sometimes felt that the earth on which he stood was but another small star, one little piece in the larger sliding nightscape. *I am part of something bigger.* Earth and sky, wolf and owl, stars and stone, dirt and bone were all woven together into an immense design.

Another signal was passed to initiate the pincer action. They were going to press the herd into a narrows so it could not spread out too far on the high plains ahead. Led by the outflankers, the packers from both the east and west flanks began to race out and press each side of the caribou herd, forcing it into the narrows. Signals flew back and forth, except now there was a nick in the pristine silence.

Urskadamus! That cursed gnaw wolf Heep was clicking his teeth as if he were gnawing a bone. The nick in his slashing tooth was fracturing the silence. Could no one else hear it? Faolan shifted his eyes to look about and nearly stumbled as his intense concentration broke. That tooth! He could not let this happen. A sly grin crawled across Heep's face, and a glint flickered in his eyes. Heep was doing this on purpose! Faolan felt Dearlea tense as she detected the break in Faolan's stride. He knew she had been impressed with him so far. Well, he was not going to let Heep wreck his attention.

Another signal passed. A *cailleach* had been identified, and the turning guards would begin to press on the eastern side of the herd to expose him. Then the two point wolves and a blocker would be sent in to try and split off the *cailleach*. But the clicking of Heep's teeth was making Faolan miss the signals. It was a constant noise in his ears, like the droning of mosquitoes during the summer moons. *He is doing this on purpose!* Faolan stumbled again. And once more, Dearlea shot him a look. Soon a *taiga* was running close behind. He had to get away from that sound. It was driving him *cag mag*.

The *cailleach* had been isolated, and the signal for the females to drop back flashed, while eight males moved forward. The endgame was the most fascinating part of the *byrrgis*. The wolves worked in relays signaled by the point wolves. There was a chance the gnaw wolves might be called to bring the *cailleach* down. It would be easy if not for the infernal clicking sound in Faolan's ears. The clicking became louder as the gnaw wolves crouched in the grass with other packers to watch and wait for the tackle relay signals. It was so unfair. No one seemed to hear the clicking except Faolan. He realized that Heep was trying not only to ruin his concentration, but to get him to violate one of the most important rules of the *byrrgnock*, which was never to break silence before the kill rush. The clicking sound was inaudible to the other wolves, but if Faolan snapped or growled at Heep, it would be Faolan who was blamed for violating the sacred rule.

I have to last until the endgame begins. I can do this. I can do this. But the clicking of that nicked tooth buzzed in Faolan's ear. He tried to transport himself to another place, any place except where he was. *Listen for the singing grass,* he told himself.

Heep moved closer and, with eyes full of treachery, opened his mouth wide to slash his teeth together. Faolan saw that broken tooth and then the snap of jaws as Heep clamped his teeth together and began to grind. The sounds scratched into Faolan's brain like splinters.

Edme looked at him in dismay. The first signal had been given for the kill rush, and Faolan had missed his cue. He sprang off his hind legs but was too late, stumbling again and sprawling flat. Edme rushed into the gap he left. Now that the kill rush had begun in earnest, the air was lacerated with barks and howls as the wolves took the *cailleach* down.

Faolan, the wolf who had risen on his hind legs like a grizzly to confront a bull moose, lay sprawled on the ground!

When he returned from the *byrrgis*, Gwynneth was waiting for him.

"How did it go?"

Faolan's tail drooped. "Well"—he might as well just get it out—"I stumbled a few times, and when it really counted, I fell."

"You fell!" Gwynneth's dark eyes blinked and she cocked her head at a very odd angle—an angle that only an owl with numerous tiny neck bones could achieve. "You!"

"Look, I'd rather not talk about it now. You had something else to say to me?"

Gwynneth swiveled her head about in a nearly complete circle, as if to scan the immediate area. The motion was enough to give Faolan a slightly nauseous feeling. Owls could do strange things with their necks, and Faolan had not been around enough of them to become used to it.

"Yes, yes, I do. I'd like to have a word in private with you. It's rather serious."

Faolan felt the marrow tremble in his bones. "Of course."

He followed the Masked Owl toward the back of a large boulder.

"What is it?" he asked.

Gwynneth took a deep breath. "You know about…" Her voice cracked, then she gulped. "The pup on the ridge, the ridge just north of the Slough." Faolan nodded. "The Sark told me that you saw it on your way to visit her, and you were quite troubled. Understandably so." Faolan nodded again. "Well, Faolan, it was my unfortunate experience to witness that *malcadh's* murder."

Murder! Faolan thought. The violence of those marks on the bones—how could it have been anything else. But murder! Truly, the story of the *malcadh* was not complete.

Gwynneth blinked. "You don't seem surprised."

"No, I saw the bones. But you saw the murderer!"

"I heard the murderer, but I did not see him or her. You know Masked Owls have extraordinary hearing. There was a thick cloud cover and I couldn't see, but I could hear the tiny shrieks as the pup was torn apart, and then the panting. It was a wolf's pants and a wolf's footfalls as it ran away. No prints of course, for it is mostly shale and rock. But how do you know about the bones?"

"The murderer was a wolf!" Faolan felt himself stagger slightly. His hackles rose in a quivering fringe. A wave of absolute revulsion coursed through him. "I couldn't get that little pup out of my mind, out of my marrow. I, too, after all, had been abandoned on a *tummfraw*. How could I see that and not think of myself? But to be murdered by a wolf!"

"Of course," Gwynneth said softly.

"I decided to make a *drumlyn*."

"A *drumlyn*? That is the very ancient wolf word for a cairn, isn't it?"

"Perhaps. I don't know. I am still new to the ways and the expressions of wolves. But I wanted to honor the little pup. So I have been going back trying to find more bones."

"Be careful, Faolan. Be very careful. It wouldn't do for you to be caught with those bones. I know how some of the wolves here regard you. They are looking for reasons for you to fail. They might whisper that you challenged the order when you jumped the wall of fire, but it's not the order you challenge, it's them. Right now, they don't know about this murder, but if they find out, they might try to blame you. I am an owl, but I understand these wolves."

"Probably better than I do." Faolan sighed. "Some actually think I come from the Dim World."

"Exactly! They are ignorant, and ignorant, superstitious wolves can be treacherous. It's your carving, right?"

"Yes, one said he could feel the heat from the sun I carved on a bone."

"They have never seen such fine carving. They can't understand it. They think a normal wolf would not be able to do such a thing."

"But what if I am not a normal wolf? What then?"

"My dear Faolan, just because you are not normal does not mean you're bad. I have no doubt that you are not a normal wolf, not an ordinary wolf. If anything, you are an extraordinary one!" She paused. "And have you built your *drumlyn*?"

Faolan shook his head sadly. "No, not yet. Something felt wrong. I wanted to protect the bones—they are so tiny—as long as I could. Maybe I have been waiting all this time for the murderer to be caught before I build my *drumlyn*."

"So where have you kept the bones?"

Faolan looked up and gazed into his friend's dusky face. There was a sudden sparkle in her dark eyes.

"Aaah," Gwynneth said gently. "With Thunderheart's paw, of course."

Gwynneth knew of Thunderheart, for it was at the skeleton of the grizzly that they had first met. The Masked Owl had been drawn there by the eerily mournful lament that Faolan howled upon the discovery of his second Milk Giver's bones. She looked at Faolan. She was sorry she had to bring him this news. His experience with the *malcadh* had been bad enough, and now this. Well, at least she was glad she had not told him before the *byrrgis*. Although it was hard to imagine how he could have done much worse. A fall! Unbelievable!

CHAPTER TWENTY-FIVE

LAST PLACE

THE *GADDERHEAL* OF THE MACDUNCAN clan was large, but not large enough to accommodate the crowds of wolves and owls who had gathered excitedly to hear the results of the *byrrgis*. So the announcement was held outside, where the owls could perch in the sparse grove of birch trees.

There was a point system in which the gnaw wolves' performances in the *byrrgis* were judged on several different aspects of ability and conduct. Scores were given for basic proficiency in running, smooth shifting in rates of speed and direction, adherence to formation, and interpretation of the silent signaling system. Extra points could be granted for certain tasks if performed exceptionally well. Even before the scores were announced, there were whispers about these extra points and who might receive them. But as Liam leaped onto a stump, the tension mounted.

"The *taigas* have concluded their scoring process. I am pleased to say that you have all performed exceedingly well in this first round of the Gaddergnaw Games. We shall begin by announcing the highest scores. In first place is the gnaw wolf Creakle from the MacDuff clan. Creakle scored a solid ten in basic running as well as another ten in position adherence. He scored five in shifting rate of speed and direction, and an additional four points in signal interpretation. Although the last score was rather average, Creakle made up for it by a powerful leap in the kill rush, earning ten extra points. With no penalties for inattention, shoving, or stumbling, the *taigas* have given Creakle a total score of thirty-nine!"

A great cheer went up. This was considered a very high score. Not as high as the legendary gnaw wolf Hamish, who became the Fengo of the Watch and had accumulated the highest score ever with an astounding fifty points.

Liam MacDuncan continued with the announcements. Second place was considered an upset, going to none other than tiny Edme, who had gained extra points for her quick thinking when Faolan faltered and for her spot-on delivery of a bite to the life-pumping artery.

Faolan, listening to the mutterings of the wolves around him, was gradually becoming aware of what a big upset it was considered that he—the wolf who had jumped for the sun—had not won, let alone placed second, in the *byrrgis* competition. A gasp swept the crowd when Tearlach was announced as the third-place winner with a score of twenty-five. Faolan felt all the eyes of both wolves and owls turn toward him.

"In fourth place, with a total of twenty-two points, is the wolf from the Blue Rock Pack of the MacDuncan clan, the Whistler."

A cheer went up.

There were only two more gnaw wolves left to place. It felt as if all eyes had focused on Faolan and Heep. Faolan began to walk away. "And now in fifth place, with no extra points for anything and a two-point penalty for inattention"—Liam MacDuncan paused—"is the gnaw wolf Heep of the River Pack."

Faolan could hear Heep groveling in the dirt, pressing the side of his face into the dirt, claiming that such a lowly wolf as himself, such a humble wolf, had never expected to win this honor. He was unaccustomed to being anything but the most humble, the lowest of the low. On and on he went.

"And in sixth place, with a penalty of twenty points for two stumbles in the last quarter of the *byrrgis*, and for missing his cue for the kill rush, the gnaw wolf Faolan from the MacDuncan Pack of the Eastern Scree."

Mhairie rushed up to him. "What happened?"

"Well, I didn't bump into you!"

"No, you stumbled and you missed your cue. If not for that, you would have tied with Creakle," she said with exasperation.

"But I didn't. I was inattentive, distracted."

"Yes, but so was Heep."

"He was?" Somehow, this surprised Faolan.

"Didn't you hear? He got penalty points for some kind of inattention."

"No, I started to walk away and, truthfully, I wasn't listening. But the thing is, he didn't stumble because of inattention."

Dearlea had come up in the middle of this conversation. "He was looking around. I saw him. I had to report it to the *taigas*."

"What was it, Faolan?" Dearlea pressed. "You were running so well beside me and then you just seemed to lose it. I could almost feel it before that first stumble."

He shook his head wearily. How could he explain something that only he seemed to be able to hear? And it might appear so minor, so trivial — like the buzz of a mosquito. The two sisters stopped walking. Mhairie stepped close to Faolan's muzzle. In her deep green eyes he saw golden flecks, *like little constellations*, he thought. Mhairie and Dearlea both tipped their heads slightly and blinked as if they had seen something in his eyes as well. For a moment, the three young wolves seemed caught in a web of golden light.

"Dearlea, Mhairie, I'll tell you what distracted me, but it might seem stupid."

"No! No!" both wolves urged. "What is it?"

"Heep."

"Heep distracted you? But he was looking around himself."

"But he was doing something else, too. Have you ever seen his gnaw-bones?"

"Not really," Mhairie said. "He's not in our pack."

"I've heard his carving is not very good. Kind of clumsy," Dearlea said.

"It isn't very good, but there's something else. One of his shearing teeth has a nick in it. You cannot only see the nick in his carving if you look closely, but if you sit next to him in gnaw circles, you can hear it."

"It's like Taddeus, our little brother. I hate the way he smacks his lips when he eats," Dearlea said.

"He slurps, too, when he drinks," Mhairie offered.

They were getting it. "But this is much worse. It's horrible. It can drive you *cag mag*. It's like a mosquito buzzing in your ears during the moons of the flies in summer."

"But he wasn't gnawing a bone, for Lupus' sake, in the *byrrgis!*" Mhairie protested.

"No, but he was making that sound. He was doing it to wreck my concentration. It has never wrecked it when I am gnawing. I'm not sure why. But when I was running, it did. And then finally, right before the kill rush, I missed my cue because he settled as close to me as possible and then opened his mouth and began slashing his teeth right in my ear. I tell you, it was like slivers in my brain. He hates me."

Mhairie and Dearlea exchanged glances.

"You've got to believe me," Faolan said. There was the heat of desperation in his voice.

"All right, we'll come to the gnaw circles," Dearlea said. "They'll be going on for the next three days." She paused. "And, Faolan, the bones you gnaw count more than the *byrrgis*. You can make up for your sixth place, in the gnawing events."

"I hope so. As I said, it doesn't seem to bother me when I'm gnawing, as much as when I'm running."

"You know why that is?" Mhairie asked.

"No."

"Well, I know. It's because you're an artist, Faolan. A true artist."

CHAPTER TWENTY-SIX

TO GNAW A BONE

FAOLAN WAS ONCE AGAIN IN A gnaw circle with Heep. But he knew he had been right in what he told Mhairie and Dearlea. The clicking sound of Heep's shearing teeth, although just as loud as during the *byrrgis*, did not seem to annoy him nearly as much. Perhaps the simple act of sharing this with Dearlea and Mhairie had relieved him a bit. Even if they couldn't hear it themselves, this was the first time he had really been able to share a feeling with another wolf since he had been in the Beyond. From the corner of his eye, he caught sight of the two sisters approaching. They were coming just as they had promised. He tried to quiet his own gnawing so Dearlea and Mhairie could hear the click of that nicked tooth.

Dearlea and Mhairie stopped on the other side of

Heep. "That's interesting," Dearlea said. "The natural shadowing of the bone might be an obstacle to some, but you carve deep." She didn't know what else to say. The lines were deep—deep and clumsy—and she did detect the nick. Now she wanted to hear it.

"Oh, I am humbled by your remarks." Heep began to screw his face into the ground and writhe in submission.

"Oh, please, dispense with such formalities. We would much prefer to watch you gnaw."

Faolan had stopped gnawing entirely and was oiling his bone by rubbing it between the webbing of his paws. Oiling had two main functions. First, it marked the bone with a wolf's distinctive odor, and second, it cleared away the bone dust from the gnawing. For Faolan, there was now a third function to be served. It offered silence.

Dearlea and Mhairie should be able to hear the click of that nick. He could tell that they were both concentrating very hard, with their ears shoved forward. Did they see the nick in the bone that Heep's tooth made? Soon, the two moved off. Heep slid his green eyes toward Faolan. Then he whispered as if to himself although everyone in the gnaw circle could hear him, "I can't imagine why two such high-ranking wolves, wolves from the Carreg Gaer, would stop to look at my humble work." No one said anything.

The gnaw wolves went on gnawing, and there was no sound except for the scrape of teeth on bone until Edme lifted her head. "Uh-oh! Here comes the Fengo Finbar," she said.

Heep immediately dropped his bone and started to twist not just his face, but what seemed like his entire body, into the ground.

"Up, up!" Finbar was a handsome brown wolf with a lustrous coat. One of his back legs was twisted so that the paw was actually reversed. "Veneration and obeisance practices are suspended during the games. They are a waste of time when such important business is being conducted.

"I am here to remind you all that you should be thinking about your story bones. In the old days, it was permitted to gnaw three, even four bones to tell a story. But during the time of our late and venerable Fengo Hamish, it was decided that it was even more challenging to be concise. So for your stories, my advice is to keep the focus narrow, prove a single point or follow a single idea, but develop it with specific examples and facts. Try to avoid clichés."

Edme raised a paw, "Pardon me, Honorable Fengo,

but might you give an example of a really good story bone that a gnaw wolf from the past has carved?"

"Aah, very good question. Undoubtedly, the very best bone ever gnawed was that of our late Fengo Hamish, telling the story of how he and the late king of Ga'Hoole, Coryn, first met when Coryn came to the Beyond as an outcast from his mother's hollow. It was not so much the events of the story but the deep feelings he expressed. It was an outcast's story of another outcast. It was as if Hamish had to get outside himself and his own agonies before he understood them and the world in which he lived. Hamish showed Coryn's agony in being an outcast, unloved, nay hated, by his tyrannical mother, Nyra, and yet cursed with a face so similar to hers that, in his wandering, he provoked fear wherever he went. The high point of the story occurred when Hamish first meets Coryn. He described the spark between them that kindled their long friendship. Simply gnawed, this bone—a tibia, I believe, from a musk ox—told a tale of profound friendship."

It was as if he had to get outside himself and his own agonies before he understood them and the world in which he lived. The words of the Fengo Finbar resonated deep in Faolan's marrow.

The Fengo cocked his head to one side and closed his eyes until there was just a slit of green light from each. He seemed to be contemplating something in the distant past. "A bone gnawed with such compassion seemed to touch the marrow of all wolves. Classic. A true classic." Then the Fengo walked away without saying another word, as if he was still in the thrall of that memorable bone.

The gnaw wolves of the circle all looked at one another, undoubtedly with the same thought. *How will I ever match that?* But Faolan was not thinking of bones or the competition at all. It was as if he had moved outside his own body. He was on that ridge again where the pup had been murdered. Murdered by a wolf!

He was trying to imagine the killer winding up that steep incline to the flat rock on the top. How long had it been after Faolan had left? If he had stayed and just kept watch over the poor little pup, would she have died before the murderer could get to her? But if he had stayed, would he have been tempted to save her? Questions whirled through Faolan's mind as the other wolves gnawed. He had thought there was more to the pup's story, but never had he imagined it would be so complicated and so gruesome.

A sleeping den was reserved for the competing gnaw wolves, but Faolan preferred to sleep alone. For even after a day of working, the gnaw wolves often talked long into the night, and the constant discussion of the competition put Faolan on edge. Although everyone was careful not to reveal too much about the story he or she was carving, they loved to discuss certain challenges they were encountering. Faolan had yet even to come up with an idea for his story, so he had nothing to reveal. He wasn't worried. He knew that, sooner or later, he would think of something. Many of the stories focused on the gnaw wolves' deformities and how they overcame them. Edme's was particularly affecting, describing how she began to understand that she did not necessarily miss the eye she was born without, but thought of it instead as hovering above her in the sky, looking down upon her and giving her courage.

Creakle insisted that although he was missing a paw, he possessed what he called a *lochin* paw that served him well and had forced the muscles in his leg to become much stronger. Therefore, he was gnawing a bone about his great leap in the kill rush that brought down the caribou.

Heep was rather reserved about his own bone, but,

when pressed by Tearlach, replied quickly—a bit too quickly, Faolan thought—that he was gnawing a bone about the unexpected joys of humiliation. "It's really a philosophical story about the strange fulfillment in understanding one's place as the lowliest of creatures and the reverence it gives one for the Great Chain that orders our existence on earth." Heep slid his eyes toward Faolan. Edme felt something seize in her marrow when she caught the treacherous glint in Heep's gaze. Had Faolan seen it?

The Whistler yawned loudly during Heep's explanation. He was gnawing a story about an early memory of when he had first found his way back to the MacDuncan clan and wondered whether it was better to live as a lone wolf. It seemed to Faolan a very honest tale, but he heard Heep snickering. "If I might humbly ask the Whistler how he could ever consider abandoning this noble clan for life as a lone wolf?"

"No," snapped the Whistler. "You may not ask. When I finish my bone and you see it, perhaps your humble mind will understand."

Tearlach seemed to prefer not to discuss his story, although he gave small hints on occasion. Faolan, however, had not given the slightest indication. When he had finally decided what he would carve, he was careful to go to the pile to pick a bone when no one else was around. He had selected a pelvis of a marmot because there was a beautiful gray crack that ran diagonally across it and reminded him of the river from which Thunderheart had rescued him. There was also a spot on the surface that was slightly discolored and in the shape of the cave that had been their summer den. It amazed Faolan that the other gnaw wolves did not take more time in looking at their bones and discovering the interesting designs that occurred naturally on the surface — small fractures, shadows, slight depressions. Heep had used the natural crack in a bone once, but only once, when he carved the image of Faolan jumping the wall of fire. That crack was so obvious, it was hard to miss. But as far as Faolan could tell, neither Heep nor any of the other gnaw wolves had looked for these features in the bones they were incising.

There was a landscape that already existed if one looked carefully, and then all one had to do was arrange one's carving around that landscape. In the pelvis of the marmot, there was river, sky, a summer den — only Thunderheart was missing, but that was what Faolan's teeth would inscribe. The story seemed to press to get out, so that Faolan's teeth almost ached with the story they held.

Late one evening a few days after the story bones had been started, Faolan saw a tree with forking branches that he felt might make for good sleeping. The last time Faolan had leaped into a tree was when he was chasing a cougar in the Outermost. This leap looked about the same distance and certainly did not require the kind of leap he had made jumping the wall of fire.

He did not even have to take much of a running start before he was in the tree with his legs draped over the fork. He had not realized it, but there were two other branching limbs that joined these from the back of the tree. It formed a sort of basket similar to the ones that Rogue colliers and smiths carried their coals in, although much bigger. It was the perfect den, if one could call such a place a den.

Faolan looked up through the black embroidery of the fringed spruce branches against the sky. The stars were just breaking, and he could see the first antlers of the caribou's constellation. It made Faolan think of the *drumlyn* he had built for the caribou he had caught nearly a year before. How different it was from the violated little bones of the pup on the ridge, he thought. Faolan shivered in his sky basket, as he had come to think of this tree den. He felt high enough to reach out and touch the stars with his paw. Those starry antlers of the rising caribou constellation were a sign that the Great Star Wolf was returning to guide the mist of the murdered pup to the Cave of Souls.

Faolan twisted around to lift his splayed paw to the light of the moon just above. There it was, the *malcadh* mark, the dim tracery of spiraling lines like a swirled star. The print on his paw seemed to merge with a whirl of stars in the sky. Once again, the thought came to him that he was part of something bigger, a larger design that was just one fragment of a single piece, an endless cycle spinning around and around like those swirling lines on his paw. He recalled that terrible night when he had found the skull of Thunderheart and howled his grief into the darkness. He remembered how he had taken some solace in the thought that, for one moment in the infinite loop of cycling time, his and Thunderheart's lives had come together. His *glaffling*, as the wolves called the howls of mourning, was as much a prayer of thanksgiving as a song of grief. The words of his mourning howls came back to him now.

Cycling, cycling forever
bear, wolf, caribou.
When had it all started, where will it end?
We are all part of one,
from such simple beginnings
and yet all so different.
Yet one.
One and again,
Thunderheart eternal,
now and forever!

But the song soon faded as he crossed the border into sleep and entered a dreamworld in which he trotted across the starry night, looking for the little *malcadh* pup to see if she was safely climbing the ladder to the Cave of Souls.

I am a star walker! he dreamed as he walked throughout the constellations, looking for the little pup. He knew he dreamed, and yet this was much more tangible than any dream he had ever had. The night air seemed billowy beneath his paws, and his silvery fur captured the flickerings of the stars until he felt wrapped in a radiant mist of light.

It is all so real! So real and so familiar. Have I been here before? But that was impossible. What living wolf had ever walked the stars? And he was not dead. A long shadow began to stretch itself across the nightscape of his dream. A shiver passed through him and it was as if the marrow in his bones shifted ever so slightly. Just then, he heard a *click . . . click . . . click . . . Not here. Surely not here!*

He awoke with such a start that he almost pitched himself from the tree. His ears were pricked up. But there was only silence, not the clicking of that nicked slashing tooth. "It was in the dream I heard the clicking," he whispered softly to himself. *In the dream!*

He looked straight up through the branches to the star-dusted night he had just walked in his dreams. He squinted his eyes so he could see the stars between spruce needles. And then it came to him, the image of those tiny bones bristling with needle-like slashes. He must look beneath the fury of the marks. Something else was there that he had not seen before. All these days that the gnaw wolves had been carving their story bones, there were bones out there on the slope with the little pup's story already told.

He could almost see the pup leaping down from the star ladder, snarling in vengeance at her killer. She would have no rest until the murderer was known. In that moment, Faolan knew what he had to do. He had to go and retrieve the bones he had buried with Thunderheart.

Quietly, he crept down from the tree. He looked up. The moon was very bright, so he worried he might be seen leaving. But he spotted an immense cloud rolling in from the east. He waited a few minutes, and when the cloud began to obscure the moon and the land darkened, he set off at a brisk pace.

CHAPTER TWENTY-SEVEN

GHOST WOLF

HEEP HAD BECOME SUSPICIOUS during the last moon, the Moon of the Cracking Ice, that Faolan was up to no good. As the close of the *gaddergnaw* approached, he was becoming more and more desperate. He knew in his marrow that his destiny was to be a wolf of the Watch. If the present king of Ga'Hoole died and a new monarch retrieved the Ember of Hoole, all the Watch wolves would be released from their duties, and, like Hamish, the great Fengo whose twisted leg turned around, their deformities would disappear. And finally, finally, Heep would have a tail. *What had been broken in their bodies was mended; what was twisted was made to grow straight; what was crippled gained strength.* This was no dream, this was no legend. This was true.

But Heep was worried and desperate, for despite Faolan's low score, there was still a chance he might redeem himself with his exquisite carving. Heep did not worry so much about the other gnaw wolves. He was a MacDuncan, after all. MacDuncans started the Watch, and every wolf knew they were favored, despite all the talk about all contenders being equally treated. It just wasn't so.

Heep had to knock Faolan out of the competition for good, and an ingenious idea had come to him a few days before. Why had he never thought of it before? He watched Faolan slip off into the night. By the time Faolan came back, the game between himself and this loathsome wolf would be over. He watched that luxuriant silver tail, like a furry comet across the night, flag out behind Faolan. Heep felt the phantom pain where his own tail should have grown. *You'll be done for by dawn,* he thought.

Heep raced some distance off in the opposite direction. There was a lone spot where three birch trees had grown together. Their trunks entwined, their roots entangled. The place where such trees grew was considered unlucky. Some said the seeds of the trees had been sown during moon rot, the time when the shadow of a previous night's moon hung in the sky the next day. But Heep did not care. It was perfect for hiding his bone, the real bone that he had begun to carve, telling the story of the murder of a *malcadh* by a wolf. Not just any wolf but a gnaw wolf! He had another bone as well. A bone of evidence.

"Wake up, Dearlea, wake up!" Mhairie nudged her sister's shoulder, then gave a good hard shove to her jaw.

"What? What are you waking me up for? Get your face out of mine."

"It's about Faolan."

"What about him?" Dearlea said wearily. "Did he carve another profane bone? I wish you'd stop worrying. The MacDuffs have always been suspicious of him. They're suspicious of everyone."

"It's not about any bone."

"What is it, then?"

"Faolan's gone off in the middle of the night!"

"He has a right to. As long as he shows up for all the *gaddergnaw* activities, he can do whatever he pleases anytime."

"In the middle of the night? It's strange, you have to admit it."

"Great Lupus, you're getting to be a MacDuff!"

"No! I just worry. He's tracking on thin ice with all these rumors. And he did it before when we were over at the Yellow Springs and I was running as outflanker."

"You saw him go?"

Dearlea was now sitting up. She shook her head violently as if to clear her brain, and yawned, but not in boredom. She stared down at her paws. Then, in a gesture Mhairie knew well, Dearlea put one paw over the other and scratched. It was a habit of hers when she was thinking hard about something.

"I know what you mean," Dearlea said. "I guess I worry, too. What is it about him that...that—"

"That makes us want to protect him?" Mhairie asked.

"Yes, I guess that's it. For all his extraordinary strength, he seems...well, not weak, but vulnerable."

"I know. And when he goes off like this, I just think he could get in trouble somehow." She paused a moment. "He goes far, too."

"How do you know?"

"I tried to follow him once. But I saw how far he was going, and I knew I couldn't make it back in time to help you and mum with the pups by daybreak."

"But *he* makes it!"

"Yes. He's fast. I've seen him come back, and he's pretty tired when he does. But tonight I thought I saw the shadow of a wolf off in the trees when he left."

"Someone we know?"

"I couldn't tell. It was only a shadow. That's what really got me worried. If one wolf saw him and knows something and with all these rumors flying around... It's kind of scary. Some wolves are just waiting for him to fail."

"Or setting him up to fail," Dearlea said.

CHAPTER TWENTY-EIGHT

TESTIMONY

FAOLAN STARED DOWN AT THE TINY rib bone, and then at the fragment of jaw he had found. He crouched down, blinked several times, then tipped his head one way and another. He looked for the landscape of this bone, but it seemed to have been obliterated by the frenzy of teeth marks. He knew that every bone told a story, even the bone of such a young pup. But there seemed to be only one story here—that of violence, of murder. Parts of the bone had been crushed and the marrow had leaked out, leaving the rib as hollow as an owl's. He looked at one of the pulverized edges and worked backward with his eyes toward the solid midsection of bone. Beneath the blizzard of marks, he saw something that froze his marrow. It was the first word of the uncompleted story—a nick. Not any nick, but *the* nick! The mark made by that broken tooth he had seen when Heep opened his mouth wide just before the kill rush began. Once again, the splinterish sounds crackled in Faolan's brain.

"Why? Why have I never seen this before?" He gasped. His marrow boiled. *Heep murdered that pup!*

Every time Faolan had come to retrieve bones, he had been staring at the evidence, yet never realized it! Now dozens of nicks seemed to storm to the surface of the bone, as if to mock him in his blindness.

Taking as many of the tiny bones in his mouth as he could, Faolan set off from his encampment at attack speed. He knew he could keep up this pace all the way back, for his anger fueled him. Hillocks flew by. He leaped streams he had once swum. A grove of birches flashed past him in a white blur. The clouds overhead, pushed by a strong west wind, were slow as sap in comparison to the silver streak that was Faolan running with love and hatred in his heart. Love for the pup. Love for what it never had a chance to be. And a deep abhorrence for the absolute vileness of Heep. The pup's story was about to end.

When Faolan was less than a league away from the encampment, he was caught by surprise by a *skreeleen*'s howl. "The gnaw wolf Faolan approaches!" Next came a high-pitched shrilling from scores of wolves. He could catch threads of words—"Dim World...*vyrrwolf*...demon wolf...witch...murderer!"

Just then, two large wolves swept down on either side of him. One bit him viciously on his hip. Other wolves pulled the attacking wolf off. But within seconds, more wolves were on top of Faolan, crushing him so he could not speak.

A mass of wolves parted as if to make way. "Here he comes. Here he comes."

Who is coming? Faolan thought. *What is happening?* But the air was being squeezed out of him and he couldn't lift his eyes to see.

"Most humbly I submit that this indeed is the murderer of the *malcadh* and I will again, with great humility since I am but a lowly gnaw wolf—a tailless gnaw wolf—submit the evidence to the *raghnaid*."

Raghnaid? *Murderer? Evidence?* Faolan listened to these oily words in terror. What evidence could *Heep* possibly have? Faolan had brought the evidence. It had spilled from his mouth when the wolves ambushed him.

Adair stepped forward and ordered the wolves off so

Faolan could stand. "Faolan, you are to be brought to the *gadderheal*, where the *raghnaid* has assembled. You are to be charged with murder!"

"Murder?"

"The murder of a *malcadh*."

"That's impossible! NO!"

Gwynneth's words came back to him. *They might try to blame you. . . . They are looking for reasons for you to fail.* And now it was all happening.

"Let the tearing begin!" A high-pitched howl went up.

"Not yet. Not yet! Wait for the judgment of the *raghnaid*!" someone barked.

Two more wolves appeared and pressed in on either side of Faolan. He felt himself carried along by a surge of flanking wolves.

"My bones! My bones!" he shouted.

"What bones?" Adair asked.

"The ones I dropped. They are MY evidence." He thought he caught a glimpse of Adair picking up the little pup's bones. But he could not be sure.

Those bones were his only hope.

When they entered the encampment, the silence was thick. Faolan was escorted immediately to the *gadderheal*. The path was choked with onlookers, and two wolves trotted ahead briskly and barked to clear the way. Faolan spotted Mhairie and Dearlea, weeping silently. He dared not catch their eyes. How had all this come about? He was in a daze as he was brought before Liam, son of Duncan MacDuncan. At Liam's side was Cathmor, looking deeply angry. She nudged her son. "Get on with it."

"Faolan, gnaw wolf of the MacDuncan clan, for the second time in less than a year, you have been brought before the *raghnaid* to answer for the accusations inscribed on a gnaw-bone."

"Wait!" He looked around frantically for Adair. "Bring the bones that I carried!"

Adair came forward and dropped the small pile. Faolan felt a momentary relief as he looked down at the tiny fragments of white. "I ask you, my lord chieftain, to look, just look down at my feet. I brought you the bones of the *malcadh* as evidence of her murder. Murder by none other than Heep, gnaw wolf of the River Pack."

"What is this?" Adair said. "Why would the murderer bring evidence of his own crime?"

"Because it's not MY crime. It's Heep who murdered this *malcadh*."

"But it is Heep who has given us the evidence."

"WHAT EVIDENCE?" Faolan roared. Two large wolves leaped on him from behind, lashing him about by his tail so that he rolled onto his back. He looked up at the wolves who stared down at him. His eyes were wild.

I must speak to them calmly. I must show some sense, exactly as Duncan MacDuncan told me.

"Let him rise," the chieftain said. Faolan staggered to his feet. The chieftain looked at him fiercely. "It is Heep who gnawed the story bone that told of..." Liam MacDuncan's voice dwindled off as his eyes wandered to the confusing pile of tiny bones.

"That's exactly what it is—a story, lies, all of it!" Faolan barked out sharply. He shoved his ears forward and held his tail straight out and rigid, in a stance of aggression as far from submission as a wolf could get. By Lupus, if he was going down, he was not going down with his tail between his legs! A sergeant at arms for the *raghnaid* came up and body-slammed Faolan so that he fell over completely. But he rose up again.

"Did Heep bring you the bones of the *malcadh*? No!

Because that is where the real story is carved, carved by Heep! Right here."

Liam MacDuncan stepped closer to Faolan and glared. "Heep brought us a bone that he will submit to the *raghnaid* momentarily — a bone carved by yourself!"

Impossible! But then, Faolan remembered the bone he had begun to carve and that had disappeared. Heep! Heep had followed him to the ridge. And the partially carved bone was his damning evidence.

Liam MacDuncan turned his head. "Come forth, Heep, and read the story bone you have carved that details the murder of the *malcadh*." Heep moved forward haltingly — bone in mouth, his eyes sliding nervously to one side as he tried to avoid Faolan's gaze, which bore into him, straight to his marrow.

"On a day in the early crescent of the first snow moon, I was heading toward the range of hills, looking for bones in the runoff. It is a good place to find gnawing bones, of which there had been few near the river since its flooding during the previous moons."

What a bunch of moose scat, Faolan thought. He had found hundreds of bones since the floods.

"As I was scouring the north face of the slopes, I noticed the recent tracks of two wolves. One track was older, and I immediately recognized it as the track of our clan's esteemed Obea, Lael. I indeed recalled that I had seen her coming back across the river as I entered on the opposite side. The other track had the distinct print of a splay-pawed wolf."

Faolan tried to protest that he knew how to run without leaving such a track. But two wolves slammed him to the ground before his first bark.

"One more outburst and I shall have you escorted out of these proceedings!" Liam shouted.

"As I continued up the slope," Heep went on, "I heard the horrible shrieks of a pup being attacked. I prayed, humbly but with great passion, that its suffering would quickly end. I thought, of course, that an owl had taken it. But I now submit this bone." He dropped the partially carved bone before the chieftain. "I ask you, has an owl ever carved such a bone?"

There was a murmuring at this last remark.

At this point, Heep began to sob uncontrollably. "Imagine my shock when upon hearing the murderer leave, I scrambled to the top and saw Faolan, his muzzle drenched in blood!" Heep, making a great effort to control his sobs, turned to the jurors of the *raghnaid* and, still gulping, continued, "Indeed, I most humbly suggest that my fellow wolves will immediately recognize the carving of this bone as most exquisite—for we all know of the gnaw wolf Faolan's extraordinary talent."

"Only a demon could do that kind of work!"

"Only a *vyrrwolf*!"

"Tear him apart as the law of the *gaddernock* declares!"

The chieftain's growl silenced the wolves. "And why did you not tell us sooner of this terrible crime, Heep?" he asked.

"I was frightened. He is a strange wolf. I believe he is an agent from the Dim World. The bones he carves are profane, but they have powers."

There were murmuring assents from a few elders of the MacDuff clan.

"That is foolish nonsense!" Faolan growled.

Liam MacDuncan gave Faolan a sharp bite.

No one noticed a lone owl entering the *gadderheal*. Owls have the peculiar ability to hold perfectly still and, with a gesture known as wilfing, shrink themselves to half their normal size. Gwynneth was indistinguishable from the shadows of flames being cast on the walls from the *gadderheal* fire pit. She listened quietly, with one eye open just a slit.

"Faolan, are these all the bones of the slain pup?"

"No, my lord. There are more."

"And where might they be?"

"I buried them."

"You buried them? Are you completely *cag mag*? Where are they?"

"I told you," Heep blurted out. "He is from the Dim World!"

"I buried the bones with those of my second Milk Giver, Thunderheart, on the north-facing slope of the salt lagoons."

But the snarling of the wolves and the call for the tearing drowned out his words. "I wanted to honor the *malcadh*. I had planned to carve the bones!"

"The murderer carves the bones!" Cathmor shrieked. "You are sick!"

"Sick! Tear him apart. Let the slow tearing begin!"

Liam MacDuncan recovered his voice. "The murder of a *malcadh* by a wolf is indeed the most grievous crime a wolf can commit, and the punishment for such a crime is that the wolf be torn apart by all the packs of all the clans, led by the Obeas. It is to be a slow tearing, as we call it. You will not receive the grace of a quick slash to the life-pumping artery. There is no *lochinvyrr* for the victim, as this is not a worthy life, nor must the meat be touched, for it is not *morrin* and will not sustain our lives.

The bones are stripped and set out for the ravens, and the bones themselves are burned, never to be carved. Is that understood?"

"Why should I dignify this question with an answer when I did not commit the crime but rather brought you the bones of that poor *malcadh* that show beyond any doubt the true murderer?" Faolan said all this in a quiet voice. His tail did not lower one bit. His ears were still shoved forward. "There is a nick in those bones. You will see it if you look carefully. You will see it on the bones I have brought and the bone that Heep put forth as evidence, as well as his story bone. But that nick was not made by any of my teeth."

A silence had fallen upon the *gadderheal* as Faolan spoke. The wolves were not sure what significance the nick held, but Faolan at least had caught their attention. Then came a rustling, and wind seemed to blow through the room. Hoarse whispers started up. "The Sark. The Sark. What's she doing here?"

The Sark lurched through the ranks of lords and clan officers. She began pacing back and forth in front of the chieftain.

"It might pay to attend to the words of the gnaw wolf Faolan." She swung her head abruptly around and stepped close to Heep, who shrank back and sank into a posture of submission. "Your 'evidence,' Heep, is very interesting."

It was only because of the mystique, the aura of unnatural power that always seemed to surround her, that the Sark was not instantly removed. The same sergeant who had body-slammed Faolan started to move forward, but Cathmor gave a silent signal and he immediately stepped back.

"Might you be so good, Heep, as to let me examine your story bone?" Heep was writhing in submissive gestures, which the Sark completely ignored.

"I offer this bone not only as art but as a testimony of a heinous crime," Heep said in a somewhat strangled voice.

"Ah, yes, testimony. You know what the word means, I assume?" The Sark continued to walk back and forth, swishing her raggedy tail. Her ruff looked as if it were being lashed into a froth by its own private typhoon from the Sea of Vastness to the north. Her bad eye had settled into a slow spinning motion while the other held steady on the floor.

"Yes, I think so," replied Heep. "I mean a humble wolf such as myself might not have the wits to appreciate the . . . the . . ."

"The subtler nuances, shadows, of the word? Is that what you were about to say?"

"Yes, yes, that's it exactly."

"Well, let me enlighten you. Testimony offers evidence of the truth. The truth, I repeat. The truth itself is not nuanced or shadowed, but evidence can be subtly altered if worked, gnawed, or manipulated." The Sark paused dramatically and then, as if she had not a care in the world, said casually, "Might I see the bone—the story bone?"

"Of course!" Heep got up and dropped the bone at the Sark's front paws. The hush was so thick in the room, one could have heard fur shedding.

"Ah!" said the Sark, rolling the bone under her paw. "A nice bone, a rib, I believe, of a moose. Generous expanse of working surface, offering a good spread for your narrative"—she paused to correct herself—"oh, pardon me—your 'evidence.'"

"Yes, evidence, Madame Sark. Along with the bone of the *malcadh*, carved by Faolan," Heep said.

"Yes, and I see here a very distinctive tooth mark made by a right lateral carnassial." She paused. "A nick! Indeed, as Faolan pointed out, the same mark as on the bone with the exquisite carving by Faolan. So both the bone you carved for your story bone and the one carved by Faolan have the same nick. Now, how could that be possible? For your story bone is a rib of a moose never touched by Faolan. But all the bones that Faolan brought have this same nicked tooth mark, if one examines them carefully." The Sark looked about, her whirling eye picking up a bit of speed in its spin as she continued to speak. "'Carnassial' is a fancy word for those back teeth of ours that are so efficient in slashing and shearing."

Faolan had begun to feel his marrow tingle and his heart race. Where was the Sark going with this?

"Almost, one could say, your trademark, right, Heep? Interesting!" The Sark paused again. "And I am sure, Heep, that you thought your biggest problem was not your teeth but your tail—or lack thereof."

Heep began to tremble.

The Sark wheeled around and faced the more than three dozen wolves packed into the *gadderheal*. "I have in my possession a tiny bone from the *malcadh* slain on the ridge. I would beg the indulgence of the *raghnaid* to please allow me to submit this bone for their scrutiny and to notice the nicked carnassial. There is a flurry of marks, so I ask that you look carefully." The Sark waited as the murmurs from the wolves in front of her died down.

When she was sure all eyes were on her, she flashed a Sarkish grin. "But aside from all this, I tell you that the gnaw wolf Faolan visited me a short time after he had passed the *tummfraw* where the *malcadh* had been abandoned. He came with the scent of a live pup on him. I saw not a trace of the *malcadh*'s blood. That fact and these bones prove beyond a reasonable doubt that—"

"What? What?" Heep leaped up.

"Hold him!" the chieftain ordered.

A gust swirled through the *gadderheal* as Gwynneth flew down from the shadows in which she had buried herself. "I was a witness to this crime. I heard the screams as I was flying overhead. There was a cloud cover, but I heard the breathing of a wolf tearing apart the pup on the *tummfraw*."

"But you didn't see anything! You didn't know it was me! It could have been any wolf!" Heep shrieked.

"Not any wolf. I heard the clicks of a fractured tooth," Gwynneth replied. "I thought nothing of it at the time. My mind was filled with the horror of the murder. But I heard that click."

"And so did we!" Dearlea and Mhairie stepped forward.

"You?" Heep gasped. "Where were you?"

"At your gnaw circle four days ago," Mhairie said. "Faolan told us how the clicking of your gnawing teeth annoyed him during the *byrrgis*, how you could make this sound even when you weren't gnawing. He said it was as bad as mosquitoes buzzing during the moons of the flies."

"And," continued Dearlea, "he said you did this on purpose during the *byrrgis* and that was why he stumbled and then missed his cue in the kill rush."

Faolan could not believe what was happening. His eyes filled, and everything before him turned wavy in a scrim of tears. His ruff quivered as his hackles rose and he felt his tail actually begin to wag. The very motion was strange and wonderful at the same time. He had friends, friends who were standing up for him, coming forward to offer the truth!

"But I would never do anything like this. Never!" Heep protested.

"Yes, you would," said the Sark. "There was a tangle of scents at the site of the murder, some more pronounced than others. They were scrambled, and it took me a while to decipher the one of the murderer, for it was mingled with that of the *malcadh*. You see, that brave little *malcadh* had fought, and as weak as she was, she drew blood, a tiny scratch but blood nonetheless. The blood of the murderer!" The Sark tipped her head toward Heep and inhaled deeply. "I've found the scent."

"The scent…scent…the Sark…a scent." Like a hissing spark from a coal, the words "Sark" and "scent" spun through the cave.

"And the scent I found was—"

As if a flame had leaped from the fire pit, a streak of yellow smeared across the dark shadows of the *gadderheal*.

"He's gone!" someone cried out.

"After him. Form a *byrrgis*!"

Oh, no, Faolan thought. *Let him go. Let us be done with him.* For Faolan did not want to hunt Heep, nor did he want to be part of the tearing. He wanted to be rid of Heep, but he wanted no part in his death.

Indeed, hours later, Faolan was relieved when the *byrrgis* returned that evening to report that they had completely lost the trail of the gnaw wolf Heep. It was, one of them said, as if the wolf had vanished.

CHAPTER TWENTY-NINE

A WOLF
OF THE BONE

THE FOLLOWING DAY, FINBAR, THE
five hundred and second Fengo of the Watch of the Ring
of Sacred Volcanoes, stood on a *drumlyn* of bones carved
during the *gaddergnaw*.

"I stand before you today," he intoned in a low, grav-
elly voice, "to announce the new members of the Watch
of the Ring of Sacred Volcanoes."

"Members? More than one?" the wolves whispered in
surprise.

"Yes, I can see your surprise, for it happens only
once in perhaps a decade that we find two gnaw wolves
at once who demonstrate the outstanding abilities
required to join our small fellowship. We are a small
order of wolves and a select one, but we are joined in a
trust that goes back to the beginning of our time. It was

an owl who led our ancestors to the Beyond, and in gratitude we pledged to guard the Ember of Hoole that lies deep within the crater of a sacred volcano. We vowed to protect that ember from any foe of the Guardians of Ga'Hoole. This trust between wolves and owls is ancient and honorable.

"Both the wolves selected were not the top point winners in the *byrrgis*, but their story bones exhibited a skill and depth of feeling that we have rarely seen. It is, therefore, an honor to introduce the two new members of the Watch.

"Come forth, Edme, gnaw wolf of the West Pack of the MacHeath clan."

Edme staggered a bit with disbelief. Her single eye spilled a tear as Finbar began to speak.

"Edme, you distinguished yourself on the *byrrgis* for your quick thinking and unerring aim in delivering the fatal bite. We see that you are not merely a quick thinker, but that your mind runs deep. Your bone made us feel the missing eye of yours that guides you like a spirit from the Cave of Souls. It was with tears in our own eyes that we read your bone."

Edme came forward, her tail held high and wagging as the Fengo placed a necklace around her neck with one small bone on it, the rest to be carved by Edme when she reached the Ring of Sacred Volcanoes.

"And now," the Fengo continued, "to announce the second member." Tears had begun to stream down Finbar's face. "On behalf of the *taigas* of the Watch, I call forth Faolan, member of the Pack of the Eastern Scree of the MacDuncan clan."

A great roar went up. Above all were the barks and howls of Dearlea and Mhairie.

"He did it! He did it!" They leaped high into the air, their tails wagging madly.

Such was the clamor, the Fengo had to bark a hush command. "Faolan, you came to the clan mistaken for a wolf with the foaming-mouth disease. You jumped a wall of fire. From the very first, there was talk of your extraordinary carving. There were baseless rumors, I am ashamed to tell you, that only a creature from the Dim World could have carved such bones."

The Fengo cut his eyes toward the MacDuff clan, long suspected to be the source of the rumors. "But we of the Watch know that such carving is a gift from the Great Star Wolf himself. Your story bone tells not simply a story of devotion but one of goodwill, conciliation, and understanding among the species with whom we share the Beyond. You have endured a level of abuse no other gnaw wolf has. You were impetuous and did not use good sense, but your dignity during these games, and your carving, make the members of the Watch feel it would be an honor to teach you and to serve with you at the Ring of Sacred Volcanoes."

Faolan walked forward and bowed his head so that the Fengo could place the necklace around his neck. There was a spark, and the spiraling marks on his paw swirled in front of him. *This has happened to me before.* There was something familiar, hauntingly familiar, about the weight and the feel of the bone around his neck.

Edme and Faolan stood still for several seconds, staring at each other in disbelief. The other gnaw wolves gathered around them and seemed genuinely happy with their success.

"Come on," said the Whistler to Faolan and Edme, who were still too stunned to bark or yip or utter a single word, "show some enthusiasm here!"

"But I can't believe it," Edme gasped. "I'm not sure I deserve it."

"Don't be ridiculous," Creakle said, limping up. "With your one eye, you see more than any of us, and not only that, your story bone stirs our marrow more deeply than you can imagine." Creakle paused and turned to Faolan. "And did not every one of us long for a second Milk Giver like yours, Faolan, when you read your story bone? How we would have loved to meet Thunderheart. You only read part of the story on your bone, but tonight I believe you are both to read them in full to all of us?"

"Yes, that is the plan," said the Fengo. "And what a night to read it is! For tonight is the first night the Great Wolf is fully visible. The Star Wolf will hear your stories."

And so it was as the first stars in the paws of the Great Wolf constellation clawed over the dusky purple horizon that Edme concluded her story, and Faolan began to read the last *gwalyds* of his.

He began in a quavering voice, "This is the story of my second Milk Giver, a grizzly bear. The word '*fao*' in both the language of the bears and wolves means 'river' as well as 'wolf.' The word '*lan*' in the language of bears means 'gift.' She said I was her gift from the river.

"I had no name for her in the beginning, but my very first memories were of being cradled in her arms and hearing the enormous thumpings of her huge and majestic heart. This sound wove through my milk dreams while I slept, and so the grizzly became in my mind not simply the Milk Giver but Thunderheart."

There were three more *gwalyds*, one for each season Faolan had spent with Thunderheart. When he finished, a hush enveloped the wolves, and oily tears ran from their eyes. Then, one by one, all of the wolves of all the packs of all the clans came up to Faolan.

Liam MacDuncan was first.

"May I lick the bone?" the chieftain asked.

"And I, too," Cathmor whispered. "I fear, young one, I have not treated you well. I will do better in the future."

"No, ma'am," Faolan replied. "You need only treat me as a member of the MacDuncan clan."

Cathmor sighed softly. "But you are a member now of the Watch of the Ring of Sacred Volcanoes."

"But I represent the MacDuncan clan. I was born a MacDuncan and shall always be a MacDuncan."

"My mate believed in you," Cathmor said, her voice breaking.

And I still believe in him, Faolan was tempted to reply, for it was as if the mist of Duncan MacDuncan surrounded him as he accepted these avowals of faith. The bone of the marmot that Faolan had carved glistened now from the tributes of the clan wolves' tongues.

CHAPTER THIRTY

A CHURNING
GIZZARD

AS GWYNNETH FLEW FAR OVERHEAD, following the footfalls of the animals below, something in her gizzard did not feel right. Despite the thick cloud cover, she was sure it was wolves, from the sound and the rhythm of the footfalls. And she was sure there were more than two wolves. The Sark would laugh at her and tell her she was more superstitious than a wolf. But she did not like what she heard nor what she saw when she broke through the cloud cover.

Her gizzard clenched with a deeper twinge. It was three wolves, all right! Heep with two ragged wolves from the Outermost.

Outclanners! Why were they tramping down this trail? There was no game in this part of the Beyond at this time of the year. It seemed as if...No! Not possible!

But Gwynneth carved a sharp turn in the sky. She must take no chances, for it seemed as if these wolves, with Heep in the lead, were on a direct path to the site where Faolan had buried the paw of his beloved Thunderheart! Heep had been there when Faolan said where he kept the bones, and now he was about to exact the ultimate revenge! Gwynneth's gizzard was churning. The wind was with her, and she flew like a hag out of hagsmire back to the *gaddergnaw* site. She had to alert Faolan.

Gwynneth arrived just as the wolves were paying homage to Faolan and his bone story. Gwynneth knew she could not interrupt this ritual and so she watched impatiently from the branches of a spruce tree.

As soon as the wolves had finished licking the bone, Gwynneth flew down to Faolan and took him aside.

"Are you sure that's where they are heading?" Faolan asked.

"I can't be sure. But do you want to take a chance?"

"No, of course not."

"We must waste no time," said Gwynneth. "You set off. I'll go tell the chieftains. They will organize a *byrrgis*, but that takes a while, and I know how fast you run. You'll get there sooner."

Faolan was off and Gwynneth soon followed, but the *byrrgis* was behind them both. Gwynneth could cover the distance much more quickly than any wolf, but as she looked down at Faolan, she was amazed to see his strong legs devouring the ground beneath him. He cut through the headwinds like a burning coal through dry leaves. *The track must be hot beneath his paws,* she thought. *Great Glaux, had a wolf ever run this fast?*

The rising moon wobbled like an immense silver bubble on the horizon, spraying a lake of dazzling light across the Beyond. Gwynneth arrived first to find Heep in a shaft of moonlight, prowling with his nose close to the ground while two ragged outclanners—one russet and one brindled with dark gray patches mixed with brown—sniffed around behind him. On the other side of the hills were the salt lagoons, but it was on this northern side that Faolan had buried the paw bones of Thunderheart.

Gwynneth went into a spiral dive at Heep with her talons outstretched. She did not intend to kill him. She knew she was too small for that, and the other two wolves would most likely attack, but she could frighten Heep or cause a ruckus, a distraction. Heep reared up, flailing his front legs. The other two wolves rushed in.

"Stand off! Stand off!" Gwynneth screeched. "By the spirit of Lupus, get out!"

All three wolves were dismayed. They had never heard an owl use wolf oaths.

"What are you doing here?" Heep demanded.

Gwynneth had alighted on a high rock. "No. What are *you* doing here? No civilized wolf comes down to this country this time of year. There is no game." She gave a long look at the two outclanners, who were growling low. Their stench was horrendous, for these wolves were known to eat one another during the hunger moons, and it gave them a powerful stink that even an owl could smell.

The wolves all bared their teeth, shoved their ears forward, and began to lower into attack posture. A signal was given and all three leaped toward the rock where Gwynneth perched, but the owl shot up into the air. How she wished she had brought her coal bucket. *Drop one bonk coal on any one of these wolves, and their pelts would go up in flames like a sap tree in the dry season!*

Then Gwynneth spotted the long shadow of Faolan

stretching across the slope. *At last!* The odds were getting more even. She rose higher in the air. *How ingenious,* she thought. *He has come from behind.* Within seconds, however, Heep spotted Faolan and spoke in an almost strangled voice.

"Ah, so you come for the endgame, Faolan?"

He's mad, thought Gwynneth. *The yellow wolf has gone mad.*

"It's not my endgame. It's yours."

"Not if I get the bones of your precious Thunderheart."

As she hovered above, it almost felt to Gwynneth that she had flown out of her own body and was observing a strange dance of tangled shadows in the moonlight. The four wolves moved about below her, growling and snapping their jaws.

"Give them up!" Heep snarled. "Give up the bones of the grizzly."

"Never," Faolan growled.

"Frightened? Frightened to walk the earth without your second Milk Giver?" Heep said.

"These are her bones; she is dead."

"And you are not, but you are nothing without them, am I right?" Heep snarled.

"No, you're wrong," said another voice that startled them all. The Sark sauntered over the top of the hill and stood beside Faolan. The two outclanners crouched into an attack stance and pulled their lips back in a grimace. But Faolan took a step forward, and then another and another, his tail held high, his gaze steady.

Like a cluster of silver stars in the moonlight, like a constellation coming down to earth, Faolan kept walking slowly but deliberately toward Heep and the two outclanner wolves. Behind him a mist loomed up. Heep and the two flanking outclanners began to tremble uncontrollably. They felt as if their marrow was leaking from their bones. For they saw not just Faolan, new member of the Watch, but a gathering of *lochin*, beginning with the chieftain Duncan MacDuncan and spiraling back in time to the very first Fengo, who led the wolves into the Beyond.

"Leave the bones of my Milk Giver, Thunderheart. Leave them now and go to the Outermost. I will not have your blood on my paws."

And Heep and the two outclanners sprang into a dead run toward the country known as the Outermost.

By the time the *byrrgis* arrived, it was too late. "They're gone, and Heep with them," the Sark said.

"Gone?" said Liam MacDuncan. "Gone where?"

"To the Outermost," Faolan replied. "Don't follow them. They won't be back."

Liam MacDuncan cocked his head one way and then another and finally looked up to see the Great Wolf overhead. "It's odd, but I feel the mist of my father here."

"Perhaps," Faolan said softly. "Perhaps."

A PRAYER

GWYNNETH RETURNED TO HER FORGE.
Faolan returned to the Carreg Gaer to begin the journey
to the Ring of Sacred Volcanoes, where he would be
inducted into the Watch. The Sark returned to her cave.

She fetched a newly fired memory jug and began to
whisper into it softly, so softly that the words were barely
audible.

"I am a rational being. I do not believe in magic, nor
do I believe in mist, or what the foolish wolves call *lochins*
and the owls call *scrooms*. But tonight under the fullness
of the Moon of the Singing Grass, I felt the ghosts of
wolves past. I believe they were summoned by the wolf we
know as Faolan. I believe that he does not know his power
or the cause of the odd spiraling marks on the bottom of
his splayed paw. Could he be what the *skreeleens* of old
called a *gyre* soul?"

The Sark drew her muzzle from the memory jug and stuffed a wad of Slough clay in its opening to plug it tightly. She did not want a single word slipping away. She poked at the fire in her cave hearth, then circling tightly three times, dropped onto her fox pelt for the night. It had been a long day. She was dead tired, and as she heard the sweet lament of the singing grass rise from the Slough, her last thought was not of Faolan but of the she-wolf Morag. How proud she would have been of this son she never really knew and now seemed unable to forget. *I hope she is well and I hope when her time comes, her end will be peaceful.*

And then, for perhaps the first time in her life, the Sark of the Slough sent up a small prayer. "May the Great Star Wolf be shining when she goes. May her journey to the Cave of Souls be short and straight. And may Skaarsgard help her climb the star ladder swiftly."

AUTHOR'S NOTE

I HAVE OFTEN TAKEN INSPIRATION in writing my books from history and from literature. I want to acknowledge my deep debt to some of these sources now. The gnaw wolf Heep's literary ancestor was none other than the fictional Uriah Heep, created by Charles Dickens in his masterpiece *David Copperfield*. Known for his insufferable humility and cloying obsequiousness, Uriah Heep truly is one of the most obnoxious characters in fiction.

Duncan MacDuncan's speech in Chapter Five, in which he explains why the wolves of the Beyond need laws, was modeled after Sir Thomas More's speech in the Robert Bolt play *A Man for All Seasons*, in which More says, "This country's planted thick with laws from coast to coast—man's laws, not God's—and if you cut them down—and you're just the man to do it—d'you really think you could stand upright in the winds that would blow then?" (act one, scene seven)

I owe a huge debt to the musician Bob Dylan. The rhythms, rhyme schemes, and phrasings of many of his songs and ballads permeate the poems in the narrative. Most particularly at the end of Chapter Nine, the song that Faolan howls is derived from Dylan's classic "The Times They are A-Changin'," as well as Gwynneth's mournful prayer at the end of Chapter Twelve.

I have always thought that writing is not a solitary performance, but a collaborative one between an author and the past—what she has read, listened to, and absorbed. The shoulders of giants are not just reserved for scientists as Newton suggested, but writers and artists perch there as well. If I have overlooked in my acknowledgments any giants, I apologize.

K.L.
Cambridge, MA
June 2010

WHAT WILL HAPPEN WHEN FAOLAN
BECOMES A WOLF OF THE WATCH?
FIND OUT IN

WOLVES OF THE BEYOND

WATCH WOLF

TURN THE PAGE FOR A SNEAK PEEK!

THUS SAYETH
THE FENGO

TWO WOLVES STOOD ON A WIND-
swept bluff overlooking an encampment where, two
days before, a contest had been concluded. Faolan, the
larger wolf, had a silver pelt and a malformed paw.
The second wolf, Edme, was a dusty, rather pathetic-
looking creature with one eye. But against the odds, they
had won the contest and would now become members of
the most elite wolf group in the Beyond — the wolves
of the Watch at the Ring of Sacred Volcanoes.

At last, after years of abuse as gnaw wolves, the
lowest-ranked wolves of all, they were able to stand tall,
their ears shoved forward and their tails stretched high
into the wind. But before they traveled to the Ring of
Sacred Volcanoes to begin their new lives, there was one
last journey to be made. The *Slaan Leat* — the journey of

farewell, the journey to make peace. It was a journey toward truth and understanding, toward reconciliation with their fate to be born malformed, a *malcadh*, a cursed one.

All *malcadhs* were cast out of the wolf clans at birth, left to die in the wilderness. Only if they made it back on their own could they win a place with their clan. And they only won honor if they gained a seat on the Watch at the Ring of Sacred Volcanoes. But from the time the first wolves arrived in the Beyond, it was decreed that all gnaw wolves must seek out the *tummfraw* where they were abandoned, before traveling to the Watch. By confronting the place where they were abandoned as pups, they would know that their days of humiliation and desolation as gnaw wolves were finished. Faolan and Edme had each been told the place of their *tummfraw*. Faolan had been abandoned on the banks of the big river that sliced the Beyond in two. For Edme, it was the northernmost peak of Crooked Back Ridge.

A bitter wind cut through the two wolves' pelts. The weather was unseasonably cold for a spring moon, the Moon of the Shedding Antlers. Both wolves looked up. The sky was sealed with roiling storm clouds, as if a blizzard was about to be unleashed. But weather did not concern them as much as this last journey. Through each wolf's mind coursed the same questions. *Will my desolation dissolve? Will I truly find peace? Will I finally belong?*

Their Fengo's words still rang in their ears. *Go forth, find your tummfraws, and know that you are cursed no more. You are malcadhs no more. You are wolves of the Watch and ready to serve. Thus sayeth the first Fengo who led us out of the country of the Long Cold and into the Beyond over one thousand years ago.*

CHAPTER ONE

UNDER THE STARS

"FAOLAN, DID YOU HAVE A SENSE of where your *tummfraw* was before the Fengo told you?" Edme asked.

"Well, I knew it had been on the banks of the river. Thunderheart told me so, but I was never sure where exactly."

"But now that you know, does it seem right?" Edme peered at him intently with her single eye. They had set out together for the first part of their journey since their *tummfraws* were in vaguely the same direction. When the sun rose tomorrow, they would each go separate ways, and then after they had found their *tummfraws*, they would meet up again and travel together to the Ring of Sacred Volcanoes.

"Why do you ask if it seems right, Edme? The Fengo must know."

"I suppose so, but I can't explain it. That peak on Crooked Back Ridge just doesn't seem to fit. I've heard that every gnaw wolf carries a sense of the place they were left to die. That the gnaw wolf has a hunch."

"And you don't?"

"I'm not sure." She paused. "But if I had, it wouldn't be the north peak on the ridge. That just seems entirely wrong to me." She shook her head, as if she was trying to figure out something disturbing.

Faolan looked at her. Their acceptance into the Watch was supposed to mark the end of their desolation and despair, but Edme seemed more hopeless than ever.

Edme was a small wolf. Of all the gnaw wolves, her outward appearance was the most wretched. Yet her bold spirit dispelled pity. She possessed a natural optimism, a good cheer that was all the more remarkable because her clan, the MacHeaths, was known for their brutality. Even now, she tried to muster some of that good cheer, which made Faolan feel sorrier for her.

"Look, Faolan — look at the stars. There's the Great Wolf pointing to the Cave of Souls. Now, what did you say Thunderheart called it?" The question was so like

Edme — full of curiosity, so ready to be interested in someone else and not absorbed in her own worries.

"She said the bears call their Cave of Souls Ursulana."

"What a lovely word — Ursulana." Edme repeated the word as if to savor every syllable.

"I wonder sometimes if all heavens are really one, if there are no borders in the sky."

"Splendid!" Edme exclaimed and began a baying song that she made up as she howled. Long resonant yowls curled into the night as constellations rose in the east, and the blackness of the night tingled with stars. Faolan listened. He hoped — oh, how he hoped — that he was right, that what Edme howled was true, that all those heavens were one. Then someday he would be united with Thunderheart, the grizzly bear who took him in when the wolf clan abandoned him and raised him as her own.

They had camped for the night near a small marsh sprigged with tiny bright yellow blossoms of beewort. The two wolves had found a place to sleep under an outcropping of rock. Across the top of the rock, a spider had woven a web, and its silk threads trembled in the night breeze. Faolan was taken by its delicate beauty. "I've heard that the silk of a spider's web is much stronger than you could ever imagine."

"Really?" Edme's eye sparkled with interest. "Wherever did you hear that, Faolan?"

"The Sark. The Sark of the Slough. She told me. She uses it to stop bleeding and bind wounds."

"You're close to the Sark, aren't you?" Edme asked in a taut voice. Faolan knew that the mere mention of the strange old wolf, whom many regarded as a witch, often provoked this response.

"Yes, she understands me in ways others don't."

"Do you suppose your mother visited her — you know, after . . ." Edme didn't finish the thought, but Faolan knew what she was asking.

After giving birth to a *malcadh* and being cast out of their clans, many she-wolves went to the Sark to recover. She had them drink potions that she brewed to help with what was called the Forgetting, so the she-wolves could move on, find a new clan, a new mate, and birth healthy pups.

"My mother, whoever she was or is, did not visit the Sark. The Sark told me so. Do you think your mother went to her?"

Edme hesitated before answering. "I have no idea, just

as I have no inkling about this *tummfraw.*" Faolan noted that Edme did not say "my *tummfraw.*" The peak on the ridge had no more meaning for her than the most distant star.

Shortly after the two wolves set off, they picked up a trail of elk headed back north with their young calves. Caribou shed their antlers during the frost moons, but elk shed theirs during the spring moons. Thus this time was called the Moon of the Shedding Antlers or sometimes the Moon of New Antlers.

Mice populations made short work of the antlers, which were rich in nutrients. But Faolan and Edme had found a few still intact and had begun to gnaw them, inscribing them with designs that told the story of their *Slaan Leat.* This desire to gnaw designs was instinctual in Watch wolves. It was not required that they bring a *Slaan Leat* bone back to the Ring. But there was a compulsion that urged them to record their journey. It did not matter if the antler was ever seen or read; they needed to mark this milestone in their journey from gnaw wolf toward a life of service at the Ring of Sacred Volcanoes.

And so they gnawed designs of the constellations floating above them and tried to describe the haunting scent of the beewort that drifted across the marsh, the quivering beauty of the spiderweb sparkling with night dew, and the low, gentle song of the grass as the wind stirred it on this late spring night.